The Oak Tree Prince

&

Other Fairy Tales

The Oak Tree Prince

&

Other Fairy Tales

N.C. Sellars

Published by Eskar, LLC

Text copyright © 2017 by N.C. Sellars

Cover design by www.ebooklaunch.com

ISBN: 978-0-692-96520-7

Printed in the United States of America

For Baby Boy and Baby Girl

(and my own babies one day)

Contents

The Wishing Coin

There once was a girl named Kerry who dreamed of marrying a prince. She thought of little else; each day she was consumed with fantasies of castles and jewels and beautiful clothes as she tended her chores. She lived with her family in a little cottage by the sea, and when she went to bed every night the fantasies continued in her dreams.

It was a tradition in Kerry's family for every girl to be granted one wish on her seventeenth birthday. At daybreak each would take a coin, throw it into the ocean, and make her wish. It was no surprise that when Kerry turned seventeen she knew exactly what she wanted to wish for. At the first hint of sunrise she jumped out of bed, grabbed a silver coin from her dresser, and raced outside. Barefoot and wearing nothing but her nightgown, she stood on the cold sand at the edge of the water and closed her eyes. She inhaled the salty air and said in a clear voice, "I wish to marry a prince." She threw the coin as hard as she could, and it disappeared into the gray waves with the tiniest of splashes. Kerry waited, ready to be transported to the nearest castle and begin her new luxurious life.

But that is not what happened. Instead, Kerry heard a loud, rushing sound. Startled, she opened her eyes and saw a woman emerging from the waves. She was formed entirely of water, with starfish in her hair and seaweed wrapped around her arms like bracelets. She held Kerry's coin in her hand, and tossed it in the air as she approached the shore. Kerry stared at her, frozen in place.

"Who are you?" she managed to ask.

The woman smiled. "I am Brenna, the spirit who lives in these waters and grants wishes to young girls."

"It's very nice to meet you," stammered Kerry, unsure what else to say.

"I have heard your wish, Kerry," said Brenna, "and it is in my power to grant it, but I first want to make sure it is truly your heart's desire."

Kerry nodded eagerly. "Oh, but it is. It's what I want more than anything."

Brenna laughed. "You say that now, but what if you were to change your mind? There are other things you can wish for. Why not ask for wealth, or fame, or everlasting happiness?"

"I don't want any of those things," insisted Kerry. "I was born to marry a prince, to live in a castle and travel to other lands. Please, please grant my wish!"

"Don't worry, I will grant your wish," said Brenna. "But first you must do as I say. Before you can marry your prince, you must learn what your life will be like as a princess. Starting today you will work in the castle. Exactly one year from now you will attend the Spring Ball, and if it is still your wish, you will be married to your prince."

Kerry considered this. True, working in a castle was not the same as living in one as a princess, but if Brenna had asked her to swim across the ocean she would have done it as long as a prince was the prize. She could wait a year. She held out her hand and Brenna returned the coin.

Brenna winked. "Good choice." The water churned and she sank slowly into the waves. Kerry heard the rushing sound again and closed her eyes. This time when she opened them she saw not the ocean, but a bustling kitchen. Bright fruits and vegetables lay in piles on long wooden tables and the air smelled of baking bread. A girl carrying a tray of roasted duck pushed past Kerry, knocking her into a woman opening the oven door.

"Watch it!" said the woman. "There's a fire in there, you know."

"Sorry," said Kerry.

The woman looked her up and down. "I guess you're the new girl. Well, what are you waiting for? Get an apron and start slicing those vegetables. And put your hair up; you're not the Queen of Sheba. We only have ten minutes before Prince Desmond wants the meat course."

This is how Kerry's life in the castle began. Every day she helped cook breakfast, lunch, and dinner for Prince Desmond and his guests. She mended sheets and hemmed shirts and threw kitchen scraps to the pigs. Every night she lay down with the other kitchen girls on a bed of hay near the fire and went to sleep, completely exhausted. Days turned into weeks, and she began to wonder if she would ever *see* Prince Desmond, much less marry him.

One afternoon in early summer the cook sent Kerry outside to fetch some water. She found the pump near the stable and began filling the buckets. She had nearly finished when a loud trumpet blast came from the direction of the castle gates. Everyone stopped what they were doing and watched as a large group on horseback rode toward the stables. One man broke off from the others and approached the water pump.

"Prince Desmond needs water for his horse," he said to Kerry. "Take those over to him." He gestured to the buckets.

Kerry hesitated. The cook had told her to be quick, and Kerry did not want to be shouted at for accepting a separate task. Filling the buckets took a great deal of time, and her shoulders and back ached from pushing the heavy iron pump. She glanced at Prince Desmond, who was even more handsome in person than in his portrait.

"I work in the kitchens," she said, torn between her desire to help the prince and avoid a scolding. "If you let me take this water inside first I'll come right back—"

"I don't care if you work in the kitchens or in the aviary," the man barked. "You work for Prince Desmond. Now take the water to his horse. Immediately."

Defeated, Kerry lifted the buckets by the handles. They were large and incredibly heavy, and she had no idea where she would find the strength to carry them to the prince's horse, pump enough water to fill them again, and carry them back to the kitchen like she was supposed to have done in the first place. But she hadn't taken two steps when something startled the man's horse. Its hind leg shot out and knocked one of the buckets from Kerry's hand. The precious water spilled onto the ground, turning the dirt to mud.

The man shook his head. "Clumsy girl," he muttered.

For a moment, Kerry could do nothing but stare. Her eyes filled with tears and her feet slid on the mud as she reached for the fallen bucket. But before her fingers could close around the handle it was retrieved by a young man with sawdust in his hair.

"The prince can wait two minutes for his water," he said to the man on the horse. He began to refill the bucket, easily pushing down the iron pump. "In the meantime, perhaps you can stop picking on servants

14

and keep to more important things, like controlling your horse."

The man glared at the newcomer. He opened his mouth like he was going to say something else, but rode away instead.

"Sorry about him," said the young man. "He's just the gamekeeper, but he thinks that because the prince invites him out on hunts he's better than the rest of us." He smiled. "I'm Bryce. What's your name?"

"Kerry," she said quietly. She felt embarrassed and more than a little useless standing there watching this perfect stranger pump water at twice the speed she had. "Thank you for your help. I don't want to keep you from your duties."

"Not at all," said Bryce, straightening up. "I'm just sorry you've been kept from yours. I can take these inside for you if you wish."

Kerry shook her head. "That's very kind, but I can manage." She lifted the heavy buckets and started toward the kitchens. "Goodbye, Bryce. It was nice to meet you."

"I'll be sure we meet again soon, Kerry," he called after her, a wry smile on his face.

And meet again they did. Over the coming months Kerry and Bryce became good friends. Kerry learned that Bryce was the head groom, though he did not plan to work at the castle forever. Once spring arrived he intended to set off on a trip around the world, adventuring and seeing exotic sights. Kerry told him about her wishing coin, and the agreement she had made with Brenna about Prince Desmond. The two of them stayed up talking many nights until the stars faded and sunrise approached.

As winter drew closer the nights became colder and colder. Kerry had a difficult time falling asleep, in spite of the warm hay and burning fire. Goosebumps covered her arms and she hugged her knees to her chest, trying to keep warm. She slept so poorly that before long her eyes were ringed with dark circles and she yawned constantly during work.

One morning, after a particularly cold night filled with ice and snow, Kerry stood at the table kneading bread, shivering and stiff with fatigue. Her mouth opened into a yawn and the cook snapped at her to wake up. Then Bryce strolled into the kitchen, and the cook's face lit up.

"You're here early," she said cheerfully. The cooks always made a fuss over Bryce and the other grooms, so long as they cleaned their shoes before coming into the kitchen. "And you look so bright and chipper—perhaps you can give our Kerry some advice on that front."

"I'm sorry," said Kerry. "I'm just so tired. I barely slept last night, it was so cold."

Bryce frowned. "That won't do," he said. "You know, the lads in the stables sleep with dogs at their sides. They're perfect for keeping warm."

"I don't think Cook would like a dog in her kitchen," said Kerry.

"Perhaps someone will change her mind," said Bryce.

That night, Prince Desmond hosted a banquet for visiting diplomats and their families. The demand was so great that everyone in the kitchen had to lend their aid. Kerry and the other kitchenhands rushed back and forth, taking food out of the oven and arranging it on platters. Beef and lamb and rabbit and pheasant, served with asparagus, leeks, onion soup, and potatoes encrusted with the finest caviar. For dessert they prepared twelve different cakes, plus glazed fruits, an assortment

17

of cream pies, and icy sorbets. The kitchen, as you can imagine, was a very busy place.

When the time for dessert arrived, the cook pressed a tray of sugared strawberries and cream into Kerry's hands. "Take this upstairs. Don't go into the dining hall, just stand behind the door and one of the footmen will get it from you."

Kerry followed the others upstairs, trembling with excitement. Even though she had worked at the castle for months she had still never seen the grand rooms that filled her dreams. As she stood on the stone steps gripping the tray, she caught a glimpse of the dining hall. The ceiling rose far overhead, so high she had to crane her neck to look at it, and the floor was covered in plush carpets so brightly colored they made the fire look dim. But the luxurious room was nothing compared to the people who occupied it. The ladies were dressed in silk gowns and sparkling jewels. The men were just as beautiful, and the most radiant of all was Prince Desmond, seated at the head of the table. His eyes shone with laughter and his smile was so bright it almost hurt Kerry to look at him.

The excitement didn't last long; once Kerry surrendered her tray she returned downstairs. Dirty pots and dishes covered the wooden tables, waiting to be washed. The contrast between the bleak kitchen and the sumptuous dining hall overhead was not lost on her. So without waiting for the cook's orders, Kerry grabbed a rag and started wiping the remains of the exquisite food into the scrap bucket. She set into her work, reminding herself that the gorgeous sights from the dining hall would soon be within her grasp, when a large black dog trotted over to her, its tail wagging happily.

"What's this?" said Kerry. "How did you get in here?"

The dog just blinked at her, tongue lolling from its mouth. The cook pushed past Kerry with a pile of china in her arms. "That Bryce fellow just brought him over," she said to Kerry. "I didn't want to agree, but he's a persuasive one. And he promised to bathe the nasty beast every week."

Kerry didn't know what to say. That night, thanks to the dog's warmth, she slept better than she had in days, but for the first time since her arrival at the castle, her dreams were not filled with Prince Desmond.

The days grew milder and the air filled with bird songs and the fragrance of flowers. The castle was consumed with preparations for the Spring Ball; the amount of food in the kitchen pantry alone would have fed dozens of families. Everyone in the village was invited; banners hung from every lamppost and the streets brimmed with music and laughter and the sound of friends making plans for the ball.

In the kitchen, anticipation ran high as well. With all the work required, Kerry barely had time to think about the ball and what it meant for her future. She never forgot about the wishing coin, though, and she lay awake at night turning it over in her fingers, fantasizing about all the changes that lay ahead. Soon she would sleep on a feather bed instead of hay, and wear exquisite gowns instead of servant clothes. She would dine on the same splendid food she had spent the last year learning to painstakingly prepare.

The day before the ball, Kerry filled her apron with bruised apples and brought them out to the stables for Bryce to give to the horses. Bryce grinned widely when he saw her.

"Congratulate me," he called. "I'm off to see the world tomorrow."

"Oh?" she said. "And where are you going first?"

"Africa," he replied. "And then the Indies, and after that... who knows?" The apple in his hand disappeared with a couple of crunchy bites into a horse's mouth. Bryce looked at Kerry and smiled. "Say, why don't you come with me?"

Kerry laughed. "Don't be absurd. You know what happens tomorrow."

"Right, your wish," said Bryce. "Well, if the life of a princess is what you truly want, then you should ask for it. But remember this: you don't have to marry a prince to spend time with interesting people and see beautiful things." He winked at her. "We cast off at ten o'clock. If you change your mind I'd love to see you in the morning."

When the last cake was turned out to cool and the final turkey salted, everyone in the kitchen went to bed. But Kerry did not sleep. Her mind would not be still. She turned over and over, unable to find a comfortable position, until she gave up completely and went out to the water pump for a drink of water. She filled her cup quickly—the iron pump was not nearly so daunting as when she first arrived—but before she brought the cup to her lips she heard a familiar voice.

"It's midnight, Kerry. Are you ready for your wish?"

Kerry looked down and saw Brenna, in a miniature version of herself, perched on the rim of her cup. Brenna pushed back her watery hair and smiled. "It's been a productive year, I see. Tell me, did you learn everything you hoped about being a princess?"

"No, I did not," said Kerry. "I learned how to pluck chickens and bake bread and rub down a horse, but that is all. I've learned nothing of courtly life, of manners or etiquette or anything I'll need to know when I marry Prince Desmond."

"Then is that still your wish?" asked Brenna. "To marry a prince?"

"Yes," said Kerry, after a small pause.

"I see," said Brenna knowingly. "Before you make your decision, I want to show you something. Look into the water, and see what may lie ahead."

Kerry gazed at the gleaming surface of the water. She blinked and looked closer. There in the cup she saw herself dressed in a beautiful silver gown with a glittering crown on her head. She saw Prince Desmond's eyes light up when he saw her, and ask if she would like to dance. She saw the wedding procession lined with people throwing flower petals and wishing them well. She saw herself eating beautifully prepared food by

22

candlelight, flanked by royal men and women everywhere she went.

Then, the image changed. The gems and silk and elegance disappeared, replaced by clothes that looked no different from the ones she was wearing right then. She saw herself in a muggy jungle, surrounded by tropical birds and flowers with seedpods thicker than her wrist. She saw the Arabian Desert with its boiling sun and starry, cold nights. She saw herself spying on elephants and lions in the Serengeti. In these pictures her hair was a dreadful mess and her face was sunburned. She was the very opposite of grace and refinement, but strangely enough, she didn't seem to care.

The images vanished, and Kerry found herself gazing at nothing but plain water. Brenna held out her tiny hand. "You've waited one year," she said. "Do you still want to marry your prince?"

I cannot say for certain how Kerry answered her. But I do know this: the wishing coin remained in her pocket that night, and as far as I know it is still there.

Fleur and the Ice King

There once lived a girl named Fleur who brought the beauty and happiness of spring wherever she went. Green grass and wildflowers sprang up beneath the hem of her dress; purple freesia, yellow buttercups, and blue cornflowers covered the ground when she lingered in one place. With the touch of a finger, a vine of trumpet flowers could creep along a garden wall, filling each crack in the mortar. Birds sang their finest songs in her presence; she knew the meadowlark's call as well as the cardinal's. Foxes and bears trusted her with their young, and when butterflies grew tired from their flight, they took rest in her hair. She loved rainstorms and sunshine equally; she never carried an umbrella, it was thought by many of her neighbors that she drank in the rain through her very skin.

Fleur was not selfish with her gift. Though she lived in a small village, she always worked hard to bring joy to others through her abilities. Little girls clamored for her beautiful posies on May Day, and garlands of roses hung over every cottage door. When a shepherd's prize ewe gave birth to twins, Fleur calmed the anxious creature throughout her labor and ensured the health of the lambs. Once, a widow's apple tree was struck with parasites and disease, and Fleur gladly lent her aid. At her touch the sap ran fresh with new vigor, and the wounded bark grew as smooth and strong as that of a much younger tree. The new fruit was sweeter than ever before, and people came from all over the kingdom to buy the widow's beautiful apples.

But not everyone could benefit from Fleur's abilities. She began to hear rumors of a castle in a faraway kingdom that never received sunlight. It remained trapped in the dead of winter, cold and barren of any new life. One afternoon, when Fleur was helping Mrs. Matthus plant her irises, she decided to indulge her curiosity and find out more.

"Have you heard of a castle surrounded by ice and stone?" said Fleur.

Mrs. Matthus looked at her. "I'm surprised to hear such talk from you, Fleur. You're too old for fairy stories."

"Mrs. Edwards and Miss Thomas sounded certain of it at the market," said Fleur. "I heard them speaking about it yesterday."

Mrs. Matthus brushed this aside. "It's nothing for you to concern yourself with, dear."

"But it is a real place?"

There was a pause. Finally, Mrs. Matthus placed her knitting in her lap. "Just behind those hills," she said, looking over Fleur's head, "there is a kingdom that has not seen the sun in years. There is no snow, no rain— only ice and grey skies."

At the mere mention of ice, Fleur's shivered. "How did it happen?"

"The king's chief advisor, a cruel sorcerer at heart, thought the king was spending too much time improving the welfare of his people and not enough time conquering other kingdoms. They had an argument about it one night when the king was up his study. The sorcerer lost his temper and placed a curse on the entire castle. He won't lift it until he is granted absolute power."

Fleur gazed at the distant hills. "How terrible," she whispered. The thought of the king trapped in his cold study without the sun to warm his face broke her heart.

"Now, don't get any ideas," warned Mrs. Matthus. "There is no Ice King, Fleur. The whole thing is a crock; it doesn't exist."

"But suppose it does—"

"It doesn't, I assure you. And if it did, it would be far too dangerous for you." Mrs. Matthus smiled and spoke in a gentler voice. "Try not to waste your time with such tales. You have a beautiful life here; there's no reason to throw it away for a foolish fable. Now, come take a look at my daylilies…"

There was no more mention of the Ice King, but Fleur thought of nothing else that day. When the sun began to set over the hills, she decided to follow it and see if she could bring it back to the Ice King.

Her journey was not easy. Each day and night was colder than the last; it wasn't long before the trees grew quiet, abandoned by their birds. The forest itself thinned, and soon Fleur found herself in a desolate wasteland. Coarse, brown grass covered the ground, peppered with bare shrubs. Fleur reached down and touched one of the shrubs, hoping to see green leaves and flowers appear, but nothing happened. What little life that remained in the plant was buried so deep even Fleur couldn't bring it forth. Discouraged, she frowned sadly at the bare branches and set her eyes on the stony mountains in the distance. She could just make out the spires of a castle nestled behind the peaks.

By the time she reached the castle door Fleur could scarcely feel her fingers. Her feet had gone numb long before, during her climb through the treacherous dark mountains. The sky was filled with ominous blue clouds that threatened ice and snow, but there wasn't a drop of moisture in the air. Fleur's breath rose in puffs of white smoke above her head as she looked up at the castle. She set her teeth and rubbed her hands vigorously to warm them, but it did not help.

Fleur began climbing the long spiraling staircase toward the highest tower. With each step she felt the temperature dropping, assuring her she was heading in the right direction. The butterflies in her hair even stopped beating their wings, unable to stand the cold.

"Go back," she told them. "I won't have you suffer for my sake." But the loyal creatures stayed.

At last, Fleur reached the top of the stairs. Her teeth chattered as she pushed against the heavy door. It creaked as it opened, revealing a large circular room in the top of the tower. There were no windows, but the room was filled with a dull grey light. It was much colder here than anywhere else in the castle; so cold that Fleur's breath could scarcely form a cloud. But Fleur wasn't thinking about the temperature. On the far side of the tower a young man sat motionless at a table strewn with papers. Like everything else in the room. he was cast in a grey light, apart from the crown on his head. It appeared to be made of diamond, though it sparkled coldly. This was the king Mrs. Matthus had told her of. The Ice King.

Just as Fleur made up her mind to approach the king, the door slammed shut behind her.

"I was hoping you would arrive soon," said a flinty voice.

Fleur jumped at the sound. She looked at the king, but he hadn't moved. The voice belonged to someone else.

"You are either very courageous or very foolish," said the voice. "I suppose time will tell which. But I must ask you, young woman: what brings you to my home?"

Fleur swallowed, determined to sound brave even though she was terrified. "I don't answer questions unless I can see who's asking them," she said.

The voice laughed. "Wise girl." A man with silvery hair materialized in front of the table. He folded his arms and leaned back, blocking the king from view. He studied Fleur for a moment. "I realize now my question was silly. It isn't difficult to tell what you think of this place. You can scarcely keep your head up."

"I feel fine," lied Fleur.

"Then why are you wilting before my eyes? No, no, my dear, you are exhausted." The sorcerer crossed to Fleur and took her arm. At his touch the tower grew even colder. She shook uncontrollably and each breath sliced into her lungs like a knife. "I have a seat here just for you."

The sorcerer conjured a chair beside the king and led Fleur to it. "I can think of nothing lovelier than a spring maiden as a queen. Why don't you give him a little kiss before you take your seat?"

Fleur shook her head, too cold to speak.

"Oh, come now. That's why you're here, isn't it? To break the spell and live in happiness all your days? Go on, little flower girl."

Fleur knew the sorcerer was only mocking her, but she had no choice. She looked down at the king. His noble face was fixed on the papers before him; in spite of the furrows in his grave brow she could tell he was a kind man who genuinely cared for his people. Her heart broke with sorrow for him. Fleur closed her eyes and softly pressed her lips to his cheek. Surprised, she straightened up. His skin wasn't cold at all, it was warm.

The sorcerer mistook her alarm for an attempt at flight. He pushed her down into the empty chair and snapped his fingers. A chain of ice snaked around Fleur's waist. Smiling, the sorcerer let go of her arm, leaving a ring of white frostbite on her skin. He held up a crown just like the king's, and Fleur realized it wasn't made of diamond, but of ice.

"At last our Ice King has his queen."

Fleur trembled as he approached. The crown of ice would not just paralyze her, but probably kill her as well. Her last dregs of hope vanished as she thought of her happy life in the village and the people who needed her. Most of all, she mourned the king she had set out to help, but whom she had only failed. She gazed at the crown of ice, and when she thought of the Ice King's warm cheek a single tear spilled from her eye.

The sorcerer laughed. "Cry all you like, flower girl. It will take much more than your tears to stop me."

But the sorcerer was wrong. If he had paid any attention he would have realized Fleur's presence was already working its magic in spite of her weakened state. You see, even the coldest rain is warmer than ice. And when Fleur began to cry, heavy raindrops started to pour on the castle. The roof, fallen into disrepair from the years of neglect, could not withstand the rain. Water leaked through several holes onto the table, onto the sorcerer, and onto Fleur.

If you have ever seen what a thirsty flower looks like after a storm, you will understand what effect the rain had on Fleur. Filled with her old strength, she leaned forward in her chair and spread her fingers over the table. Vines of ivy and wisteria stretched and wound their way down the table legs and across the floor. Before the sorcerer realized what happened, the vines had rooted him to the stone. The ice crown he had intended for Fleur fell to the floor and was immediately shattered by a rope of trumpet flowers.

The rain grew warmer and warmer until it rivaled a summertime cloudburst. Working quickly, Fleur reached toward the floor and drew a maple sapling from the newly sprouted grass. She encouraged it to grow until the branches broke through the roof. More rain poured into the tower, soaking the plants. White moonflowers and morning-glory climbed the round walls, crumbling the stone. The chain around Fleur's waist melted into a puddle, and as soon as she was free she snatched the crown of ice from the king's head.

"No!" shouted the sorcerer.

The icy crown was so cold it burned Fleur's hands. She threw it against the wall, where it exploded into a thousand pieces. Behind her, the sorcerer cried out in rage once more. He tore angrily at the vines, attempting to free his legs.

"Monster!" he screamed, swatting at the flock of blackbirds that descended from the newly opened ceiling. They swarmed his face, beating their wings so loudly Fleur could hardly hear his insults. "Only a monster could do this!"

More saplings sprang from the stone floor. Apple trees and pear trees and lemon trees, and rose bushes of every color. Rabbits and hedgehogs burrowed out of the walls, and Fleur heard the low growl of a bear approaching from the stairs. The rain slowed as silkworms and caterpillars wove a stiff cocoon around the sorcerer. Moss and cobwebs covered his legs, and a pair of wolf pups raced into the tower, barking shrilly and wagging their tails.

The sun broke through the clouds, sending a flood of yellow light into the tower. The pillar of spring plants and chrysalis that was once the sorcerer shuddered violently. Warmth filled the tower, and every petal and leaf took on the bright, super-real colors that follow a rainstorm. With one final burst of light, the pillar collapsed. The vines retreated and the silkworms pulled back their handiwork. All that remained of the sorcerer was a pile of glittering white dust.

Fleur's pounding heart slowed as she watched the white dust blow away. One of the wolf pups whined at her feet. She picked it up and hugged it to her chest, unable to believe it was all over. In the excitement she had nearly forgotten about the king, until she heard him speak.

"Excuse me."

The young king rose from his seat at the table. He took in the dramatic sight of his prison tower with wide eyes. With its flowerbeds and rosebushes, it resembled a garden more than a castle. Honeysuckle and grapevines covered the walls, and brightly colored birds darted among the saplings. But what struck him to the heart was the girl standing on the new carpet of plush moss and thick grass, cradling a wolf cub in her arms. Butterflies brighter than jewels shone in her hair, and he thought he saw a garden snake slither out from the hem of her dress.

"Did you do this?" he asked, amazed. "Did you break the spell?"

Flushed with embarrassment, Fleur nodded.

"My name is Nathanial," said the king. "I never thought I would see the sun again, and you brought me the entire month of May." The king was quiet for a moment. He glanced around the room with a frown on his face, as though trying to recall a dream. He raised his hand and lightly touched his cheek, where Fleur had kissed him. "Will you please tell me your name?"

The wolf pup rubbed its wet nose against Fleur's chin. Laughing, she placed it on the ground, where it began playing with its brother. "My name is Fleur."

"Fleur," the king repeated. He said it slowly, and a smile spread across his face. He held out his hand. "The perfect name for a maiden of spring."

A warm breeze swept through the ruined tower, heavy with the perfume of flowers. The blackbirds took flight once more, disappearing into the clear blue sky. The remaining shards of the icy crown melted in the grass. Fleur looked at the king, drinking in his noble face and kind eyes the same way she drank in the rainwater and sunlight. She placed her hand in his, and as she did so, every rose in the tower darkened to a deep, blushing pink.

Some time later Fleur and Nathanial married, and they reigned as king as queen for many years. They were kind and fair, and served their subjects with joy. Commoners and royalty alike came from faraway lands to visit their kingdom, which was said to be the most beautiful in the world.

The only scar that remained from the sorcerer was the frostbite on Fleur's arm. The place where the sorcerer had touched her turned from white to stony grey. During their years together King Nathanial sought every cure for his wife's frostbite, but none was ever found. The dark ring remained around Fleur's arm for the rest of her life. But it never caused her pain, for even the cruelest winter will always be defeated by the warmth and light of spring.

Cassia and Pearl

A long time ago there was a large castle on a green hill, and in this castle lived a princess named Cassia. She took lessons from the finest tutors in the kingdom and cultivated many talents. Over the years Princess Cassia grew into a kind, gracious young woman.

Unlike her friends who loved attending feasts and balls nearly every night, Cassia was happiest when she spent time with her pet fox, Pearl. Pearl had been a gift from the king and queen on Cassia's birthday, and she never left Cassia's side. Her soft fur was the color of fresh snow, apart from three black spots on the scruff of her neck. Cassia spent many a pleasant afternoon in the castle gardens sitting in the shade of the willows with Pearl curled up in her lap, scratching the fox behind her ears or under her chin.

The Autumn Festival was approaching; a week of games, races, and celebration of the harvest, all culminating with a dance at the castle. Princes and noblemen came from faraway lands to offer to serve as Cassia's escort for the festivities, but due to the formality of court life, Cassia could never tell if their flattering words were rooted in genuine affection or their own ambitious hopes.

One night after a particularly disappointing dinner with an eligible duke, Cassia lay in her bed, unable to sleep. "This isn't working," she said to the ceiling. Pearl, who was stretched out at Cassia's feet, pricked her ears and blinked her round eyes. "How am I supposed to know who truly cares for me from those who just want to attend the festival with a princess?"

Cassia thought for a moment. When she was young her nurse had read her fairy tales about princes and princesses who put on disguises and ventured out into the world so they could find out others' true intentions. But Cassia wanted more. Anyone might show kindness to a well-spoken stranger; she wanted to see how people treated something smaller and weaker than themselves. An animal, perhaps.

A smile spread over Cassia's face as she looked at Pearl. The fox's mouth opened into a wide yawn, revealing a little pink tongue inside her black maw. Inspired, Cassia leapt out of bed. She gathered Pearl in her arms and slipped from her room, heading in the direction of the servants' quarters. Padding softly down the hall, Cassia stopped before the bedroom belonging to her maid, Holly, and rapped her knuckles lightly on the door.

When Holly opened the door and saw the princess, she bowed. "What can I do for you, Your Highness?"

Cassia replied, "I wanted to ask you a favor, Holly. You told me that you're leaving in the morning to spend a few days with your family, isn't that right?"

Holly nodded. "It is, Your Highness."

"And they live some distance from here?" said Cassia.

"Yes," said Holly. "They have a farm on the edge of the forest. About fourteen miles to the east, as the crow flies."

Cassia stroked Pearl's fluffy head. "Wonderful. If you don't mind, Holly, I would be very grateful if you brought along a temporary gift. From me."

The next morning the herald issued a decree that all able-bodied citizens should gather before the castle at sunset for an announcement from Princess Cassia. Dispatches were sent to neighboring kingdoms as well, and by late afternoon the courtyard was filled to the point of bursting with villagers and royal messengers alike. Brightly colored standards emblazoned with eagles and bears and lions and unicorns fluttered in the breeze. The air itself teemed with anticipation; Princess Cassia was not known for her public appearances. Anything she had to say must've been of great importance.

Cassia stood at the edge of the balcony, just out of sight as her herald announced her. She was a little surprised at her own boldness, but once the herald finished his introduction she gathered her nerve and stepped into view. The crowd burst into cheers; Cassia waved with a benign smile fixed on her face until the noise died down.

"I thank you all for your great kindness," Cassia called, her voice echoing in the courtyard. "I truly have the noblest subjects and allies in all the world, to receive such support as this in my time of need."

Everyone waited in respectful silence. Cassia took a deep breath, then continued: "I am afraid I have lost a very dear possession of mine, and I greatly desire its return. Many of you have seen my white fox, Pearl, wandering the castle grounds. It seems Pearl ran away some time in the night. She is not a wild fox; she doesn't know how to fend for herself outside these walls. Anyone who learns of her whereabouts in the coming days is encouraged to report to the castle."

Here Cassia hesitated. She hadn't slept a wink the night before, so busy was she coming up with this plan, but she was still afraid of its potentially disastrous results. She closed her eyes, and before she could change her mind, she called out, "Furthermore, whichever man successfully returns my fox to me will attend the Autumn Festival as my escort."

Several people gasped, and a wave of murmuring broke out in the crowd. Without another word Cassia turned on her heel and left the balcony. The doors closed behind her; she ignored the stares of the servants and returned to her room. She looked at the clock on her writing desk. By this point Holly had reached her family's home and was preparing to release Pearl into the forest. Cassia had not lied: Pearl was in no way equipped to deal with life outside the castle walls. But she was an excellent judge of human character and would never put her trust in anyone less than admirable. With the independence of a cat and the affectionate nature of a dog, Pearl was fiercely loyal to Cassia. If any creature could find her way into the care of a good man, it was Pearl.

Now Princess Cassia could only wait.

Over the coming days the castle was flooded with men of all stations carrying foxes. Some were red, some were black, some were almost exact replicas of the true royal fox. But even the purest white foxes all lacked the trio of black spots that were Pearl's distinctive marks. Each hopeful suitor was sent away with disappointment in his eyes, while Cassia's patience wore thin and she grew increasingly worried about Pearl.

Pearl, for her part, was not having an easy time. The forest's muddy floor and nasty cobwebs made for uncomfortable travel, and she could not understand why she had been sent away from her home of soft carpets and warm pillows. It wasn't long before her beautiful white fur was matted with rough burrs and stained with mud. The few people she encountered were not of a kind sort, either. Horrid children threw stones at her and called her a dirty rat. She passed farms with frightfully large dogs that barked like they wanted to eat her up, and women who chased her off with brooms because they thought she was after their chickens.

As the days passed, Pearl stopped thinking about her soft bed in the castle and turned her thoughts to a more pressing subject: food. Water was not a critical issue; she encountered no shortage of streams (and one wide creek she had to wade across, much to her chagrin), and though she saw many fish splashing about she could not catch one. She stuck her paw in the water several times, hoping to flip one out onto the bank, but failed each time. The fish only laughed at her; even the birds cackled in mirth from their high branches.

One evening, just when Pearl was so hungry she thought she might die of starvation, she smelled meat. Meat! Her mouth watering, she followed the scent until she came upon what appeared to be a large hunk of roasted rabbit. If she wasn't so hungry she might've stopped to consider the strange coincidence of coming across such carefully prepared meat at the forest's edge, but all she cared about was the idea of a full stomach. So intent was she on her prize that you can imagine her utter shock when, just as she was about to reach the rabbit, a wire cage clapped shut around her. A pageboy ran out from behind a tree, grabbed the cage, and carried it away.

The pageboy was in the service of Prince Leopold, who lived in a nearby kingdom. An expert hunter and long admirer of Cassia, he had set the traps just after her announcement in hopes of winning her hand. He was not, it has to be said, a gentle prince; his people often complained of his taxes, which were raised more often than not to finance aggressive campaigns against weaker kingdoms. When the pageboy reached Prince Leopold's camp, he bowed low and placed the cage on the ground. The prince smiled widely.

"What a fine treasure you've found, lad!" Prince Leopold tossed the boy a coin and motioned for the cage to be lifted onto a table. He put his handsome face close to the cage and studied Pearl through the wire. "I daresay this little rodent is the real thing, though it's certainly not much to look at right now."

Pearl did not appreciate this. She had never seen this man before and knew nothing of his politics, but she recognized a person with a cruel character when she met one. She bared her fangs and retreated to the far corner of the cage, her hackles raised, but Prince Leopold merely laughed.

46

"Such a vicious little creature! Much like your mistress, I suppose. You'll have to learn to hold your tongue, as will she. Yes, I've heard about your princess. She can be clever all she likes now, but once she's my wife she'll learn her place. I have no interest in petty games and challenges. First, though, I must bring you to her door."

He opened the cage and reached inside, but before he could take hold of her Pearl clamped her teeth around his finger as tightly as she could. The prince swore and yanked out his hand too quickly, knocking the cage to the ground. Pearl darted out and ran through the trees as fast as her little legs could carry her. She heard shouting behind her, from pageboys and servants and mostly Prince Leopold, but she kept running. Soon she heard loud footsteps; they had almost caught up to her. To her left lay the river, large and swift. She could barely swim and knew she might drown, but she had no choice. Without looking back, she leapt into the river's icy depths and let the current sweep her away from Prince Leopold.

Later that day, a young farmer stood in the water near the riverbank and cast his net. Here the river was slower and wider, and thick with fish. The farmer's name was Owen, and though he was poor, he was very happy. The men and women who worked on his farm loved him, for even though he could not afford to pay them great wages he filled their pantries with fruits and vegetables and eggs and milk, and the occasional fish. The widows were especially fond of him, and knew they could always count on him to repair a leaky roof or mend a broken fence. Or, in a lesser degree of need, to open a stubborn jar of pickles.

Owen drew in his net and glanced at the bank. His basket was nearly bursting with fish, so he decided it was time to go home. When he looked inside his net, however, he nearly dropped it in surprise. There, among the flopping silver fish was a bundle of what looked like fur. He touched it gently and realized it was a fox. Half drowned and covered in rough mats, but a fox still. Very quickly, Owen gathered his net and fish and waded to the shore. He took off his coat and bundled Pearl into the warm folds, and then tucked her up under his arm.

"You'll be all right," he murmured. "Once you've warmed up and have got some food in you, you'll be as good as new. You'll see."

It was quite dark by the time they reached Owen's house. Pearl remained still and quiet as Owen set her before the hearth and lit a fire. She didn't mind the threadbare carpet or that the house was small; she was just glad to be indoors and out of that dreadful river. Happier still was she when Owen cleaned a fish and roasted it over the flames. Owen put the fish on a plate and cut it up into pieces small enough for Pearl, then prepared his own dinner. He watched with mounting curiosity as Pearl daintily ate her food.

"You're the strangest fox I've ever seen," he said. "You're somebody's pet, I'll warrant. Tomorrow I'll clean you up and we'll see about returning you to your proper owner."

Since he was a farmer, Owen had been working the day of Cassia's announcement, and therefore knew nothing about the lost royal fox or the reward that followed her restoration. But don't worry, everything will be revealed in its proper place and time.

It took several days (and almost as many baths) for little Pearl to fully recover from her unfortunate adventures. She spent most of her time sitting before the fire, trying to keep warm, or eating more delicious fish. At night she slept in the farmer's bed, and though it wasn't nearly as plush or heavenly as Cassia's, it was still a bed. She watched through the window as Owen went about his daily business, tending his fields and crops. She liked the gentle, honest way he spoke with his neighbors, and the way he presided fairly over disputes. He may not have held the title of a prince, but he certainly had the bearing of one.

One afternoon Pearl decided it was time to venture outside. She stayed close to the house, but sniffed contentedly along the outer walls. She played in the grass and swatted at a bumblebee for a while, and then chewed on some flowers. She even found a little green lizard and was just gathering her courage to give it a good poke when she heard a young girl call out.

"Mother! Come look at the pretty fox!"

The fur on Pearl's back stood up straight. Her encounters with children outside the castle had not been pleasant. The girl rushed to her, but instead of chasing her off she dropped to her knees and stroked Pearl's head. The girl looked at Owen, who was just coming from the fields with a hoe slung over his shoulder. "Is she yours?" she asked him.

"I found her just over a week ago," he said. "Neither of you happen to know who she belongs to, do you?" He looked between the girl and her mother.

The girl shook her head, but the mother's face turned white. "You said you found her?" she asked Owen. When he said yes, the mother put her hand to her heart. "Good gracious, this must be the royal fox."

"Royal fox?" said Owen.

The mother told him the story of Cassia's announcement. When she finished, she looked at Pearl with wide eyes. "She has the correct markings and everything. She belongs to Princess Cassia. You must return her to the castle."

"Then you can go to the festival with the princess!" said the girl.

"I don't know about that," said Owen, a furrow in his brow. "I'm only a farmer. Nevertheless, if the fox belongs to her I'm sure she misses it very much."

The girl's mother was a soft-hearted romantic, and the prospect of humble Owen being with a princess was almost too much. She could hardly contain herself. "Don't be ridiculous," she said, rushing into the house without invitation. "You're a kindhearted man, and if she can't see that she doesn't deserve you. If you leave now you'll be at the castle by nightfall. Bathe quickly and put on some good clothes, for heaven's sake. I don't care how handsome you are in the country, you can't go to the castle smelling of fertilizer."

The sun had nearly set by the time Owen reached the castle courtyard. It was crowded with carriages and carts and merchants packing up for the day. Owen kept a tight grip on Pearl as they wove through the crush of people. More than one person pointed at the fox in his arms, muttering that it had to be an imitation, but he ignored them. As nervous as he felt, his excitement grew with each step he took. Perhaps Princess Cassia would not mind his low station and lack of title. He tried not to let his imagination run away with him, but it was difficult. If you have ever been so excited about something that your heart pounds eagerly in your chest and you temporarily forget to breathe, then you understand how Owen felt.

But Owen was not the only excited person in the courtyard that day. Lingering in the shadows near the castle doors was Prince Leopold. Ever since he lost Pearl in the forest he had taken up a post outside Cassia's home. He knew it was only a matter of time before someone brought in the lost fox; he still hadn't given up hope that he might be the one to return it, even if it meant lying his way to victory.

When Prince Leopold spotted the fox, he was pleased. The man carrying it was obviously not royalty, and no sword hung from his belt. Prince Leopold stepped in the man's path and cleared his throat.

"Pardon me, my lad, but I'd like to inquire about the fox you are carrying. Is it in fact the lost fox belonging to Princess Cassia?"

"I believe it is, sir," said Owen.

Prince Leopold smiled. "How relieved she will be. Princess Cassia has been terribly distraught over the poor thing. Hand the creature to me and I'll see that it's properly returned." He held out his hand. Pearl growled at him, and Owen looked at Prince Leopold, surprised.

"I don't understand," said Owen. "I'm the one who found the fox—"

"And your assistance is greatly appreciated," said Prince Leopold. "But you must understand, my good man, that the Princess extended her challenge to men of royal lineage. Surely you didn't think she would attend the festival with any man off the street just because he caught a fox!"

Owen frowned. He wasn't sure if Prince Leopold was telling the truth. He didn't want to give up so easily, but he also didn't want Princess Cassia to be miserable at the festival, forced to dance with a poor man.

Prince Leopold smiled harder, as he always did when he lied. "Let us be gentlemen. We both obviously want what's best for Princess Cassia, and I think we can both agree she deserves the kind of company only a prince can give her."

He held out his hand again, and Owen stared at it. Prince Leopold's hand was smooth, with minor calluses from swordplay and gripping his horse's reins. It was very much the hand of a prince. Owen looked down at his own. In spite of his best efforts to wash, the lines were still caked with dirt from years of labor, and his skin was rough and sunburned. Princess Cassia would probably shudder when she saw it, much less felt its touch.

A lump rose in Owen's throat as he surrendered the fox. Prince Leopold tried not to look too pleased, though he silently congratulated himself on the success of his ruse. "You're an intelligent man," he said to Owen. He reached into his pocket and pulled out a handful of gold coins. "For your help."

Owen waved the coins away. "I don't want your money," he said, already doubting his decision. "And I don't wish to be patronized. Just take care of the princess."

"Of course, of course," said Prince Leopold, turning away. He had already half-forgotten about Owen; instead his mind was fixed on Princess Cassia. He imagined her throwing herself at his feet in gratitude, thanking him again and again for the safe return of the fox. They would marry as soon as the festival ended and she would sit beside his throne, as perfect and lovely as a sculpture. The guards opened the doors for him. Pearl wriggled in his arms, trying to leap down and return to Owen, but Prince Leopold did not let go.

Inside the castle, Cassia sat in the banquet hall at the head of the long wooden table, feeling particularly sour. She had just finished dinner with her court and a few visiting princesses, and her guests were trying to decide whether to play cards or go for a twilight walk in the gardens. Cassia wanted neither; in fact, if her friends made one more joke about her failed challenge she was going to send them away and just go to bed. But even that wouldn't satisfy her. Her empty rooms reminded her of Pearl's absence.

Princess Violet's laughter shook her from her reverie. "Come along, Cassia. Let's go for a walk while there's still some light. The fresh air will make you feel better, I promise."

"I'm quite all right," said Cassia. "Why don't you go ahead, I'll be right there—"

Suddenly, the door opened. Prince Leopold entered, escorted by a castle guard. Cassia froze when she saw the fox in his arms.

Prince Leopold bowed. "I am Prince Leopold, Your Highness. I have journeyed long and far to reach you, but now that I see your lovely face the trouble seems like nothing but a dream. I have brought your fox home."

Cassia studied him. He was handsome, just like every other prince she had known, and he was certainly dressed like one. But there was something about his features that didn't quite match the warmth in his voice. She ignored the delighted whispers from her friends and smiled graciously at Prince Leopold. "Come with me, sir, and you may tell me the tale."

Cassia led him from the banquet hall to the drawing room. A fire burned in the fireplace, casting a warm glow on the portraits covering the walls. Cassia sat on the edge of the sofa, though Prince Leopold remained standing. For the first time in many weeks, Cassia smiled.

"Thank you so much for bringing Pearl back to me," she said, stretching out her arms. "I have missed her more than you can imagine."

Though Pearl squirmed in his arms, Prince Leopold kept hold of her. "Yes, I believe you, Princess. But there is still the matter of payment."

There was a pause. Cassia's suspicion increased. "Indeed, sir," she said slowly. "I assure you everything will be taken care of in due course. Now please give me my fox," she said, irritated at having to ask twice.

Prince Leopold relented and placed Pearl on the carpet. The fox practically sprinted into her owner's arms. Cassia stroked her velvety fur, relieved that the madness had finally reached an end. She looked up at Prince Leopold. "She appears well fed and cared for. Thank you, again."

"The pleasure was mine, Princess," said Prince Leopold. "It's a gorgeous animal." He reached forward to pat Pearl on the head, but the fox's hackles rose, a deep growl pulsing in her throat.

Cassia frowned. "She doesn't seem to like you very much," she observed. "If you don't mind my asking, Prince Leopold, how exactly did she come into your possession?"

Prince Leopold opened his mouth, ready to lie, but before the words left his mouth the door flew open. To his surprise, Owen darted into the room. He had obviously been running, and when he saw Cassia he stopped. Two guards burst through the door behind him and started to drag him away.

"Princess!" shouted Owen. "Princess Cassia, I have something to tell you!"

Prince Leopold laughed. "Don't waste your time with this fool," he said uneasily. "He's obviously out of his mind."

"It's about your fox!" called Owen.

Cassia held up her hand. The guards, who had almost reached the door, stopped. "Release him," she ordered. "Let him speak."

Again, Prince Leopold laughed. "Really, Princess, this isn't necessary—"

"Let him speak," she repeated. The guards backed toward the wall as Cassia approached Owen. He had an open, honest face, and his stature suggested a life of laboring in the fields. But in spite of his dirty clothes she could see inner nobility. This was confirmed when Pearl squirmed out of Cassia's arm and rushed to Owen, barking happily. "What is your name?" Cassia asked, curious.

Owen bowed deeply. "My name is Owen, your highness." Pearl continued to bark, pawing at Owen's feet. Owen stooped to pick her up. "I believe this creature belongs to you." He placed the fox in Cassia's arms, and the two of them smiled at each other.

Prince Leopold did not like this at all. He had not schemed and plotted his way to a private audience with Princess Cassia just to lose his prize to a farmer. He stepped forward, a forced grin marring his face. "Thank you, Master Owen, but I believe the princess would agree your assistance is no longer necessary."

At the sound of Prince Leopold's voice, Pearl began to growl again. Cassia glanced at him. "I want to hear what he has to say. Please, Owen, tell me how you became such fast friends with my dear pet."

"I found your fox in the river last week," Owen explained. "I could tell she was domestic, and I brought her to my farm and cared for her until she was well again. Once I found out she belonged to you I made my way to the castle. But when I encountered Prince Leopold I allowed him to convince me that he was the worthier victor." He hesitated. "I apologize if I have made things difficult—you deserve to know the truth."

Cassia narrowed her eyes. "Is that indeed what happened?" she said to Prince Leopold.

"What difference does the sequence of events make?" he said, all laughter gone. "I don't appreciate trickery, your highness. I find it base behavior for a princess."

"The only person who has tried to trick anyone is you," said Cassia. "You cheated, and therefore your presence here is forfeit. Please be on your way."

Prince Leopold did not move. "This is unfair, Your Highness," he said, growing angrier by the second. "I may have solicited help from this peasant but that does not alter the outcome of the contest. I am the true winner!"

Owen put out his hand. "Your quarrel is with me, sir," he said firmly. "There's no reason for you to raise your voice at the princess."

"You gave your word!" shouted Prince Leopold. "You promised to attend the festival with whichever man brought your precious little beast back to you. I am that man, and I will claim my prize."

He charged forward, but Cassia, who was truly beginning to regret this enterprise, called for the guards. They took Prince Leopold by the arms and pulled him away. His voice carried down the hall long after he disappeared from sight.

When it was finally quiet, Owen turned to face Cassia. "Are you all right, Princess?"

"A little embarrassed, but fine otherwise," said Cassia. She knit her brow. "I'm terribly sorry, Owen. You must think I'm quite foolish. I certainly do."

"On the contrary, I think you're very clever," said Owen. He bowed once more. "I suppose you'll want to return to your guests, Your Highness. It was truly an honor to meet you. I will never forget this day." He lifted Cassia's hand to his lips and gently kissed it.

He started toward the doors, determined not to look back. Cassia watched him and, filled with the same frightened excitement she felt the day she made her announcement on the balcony, called after him.

"Wait, please."

Owen's heart filled with hope as he turned slowly. To his pleasure, Cassia was smiling. She placed Pearl on the carpet, then extended her hand to him.

"Do you not wish to claim your reward?" she said. "The Autumn Festival begins tomorrow."

"But, Your Highness," said Owen, his face turning red, "surely you don't wish to attend with a farmer."

"I said I would go with whichever man returned my dear Pearl to me," said Cassia. "Royalty was never a requirement."

"But you're a princess," said Owen. "You should be with a prince."

"I disagree," said Cassia. "You are brave and valiant, and you showed kindness to both me and a helpless creature with no thought to your personal gain. I can think of nothing more princely than that."

And they both had a delightful time at the festival, just as Princess Cassia had hoped.

The Tulip Bulb

In a village not too far from here there was a flower bulb named Tulip. She lived in a basket with her brothers and sisters at the market, and she was very happy there. She had spent all of spring and the first few weeks of summer watching people buy beautiful flowers to plant in their flowerbeds, and she was eager to go home to her very own garden. During the long, bright days of July and August more and more people wandered over to the basket, and searched through it for the perfect bulb. Tulip and her siblings always lay very still and quiet, behaving their best in hopes of being chosen. It was exciting whenever one of Tulip's siblings was selected by a shopper, but in her heart Tulip began to feel discouraged. It would soon be past the time for planting bulbs, and still no one had chosen her.

Finally, on a bright sunny morning in early October an elderly woman walked into the flower market. Most of Tulip's brothers and sisters were already gone, so Tulip lay quietly in the bottom of the basket, not very optimistic. She was starting to sulk, thinking, *I'm never going to be planted*, when the woman scooped her up in her hand and bought her. Tulip was excited beyond words. She rode in the woman's car quite happily, singing along with the radio and imagining what it would be like to be planted. Once they reached the woman's house, Tulip waited in the garage for a while and looked around while the woman changed into her gardening clothes. Tulip noticed a bag of fertilizer and thought it looked delicious.

Am I planted yet? she thought. *Is this what it means to be planted?* But then the woman came out into the garage and picked up Tulip, along with her trowel and gloves, and walked to the flowerbed in the front yard.

Tulip had never seen so many beautiful flowers in one place. There were azaleas, rosebushes, and daisies, all in full bloom. There was also a juniper shrub and a heath nearby. Tulip lay quietly in the grass while the woman dug a small hole and aerated the soil around it. Then she carefully placed Tulip inside, right side up, and filled in the dirt. The hole was deep and she felt quite snug in the warm soil. It wasn't long before Tulip grew thirsty, and she was relieved when the woman gave her a drink. The sun would be setting soon, and Tulip was exhausted from her long day. She was just settling down for a little rest when she heard someone speak.

"Did you see that rock the woman planted? What does she think will grow from a rock?" asked one of the daisies, whose name was Mrs. Popple.

"I don't think it was a rock," replied another daisy named Annabelle. "It looked more like a dirty onion to me."

It took Tulip a moment to realize they were talking about her. "Excuse me, but my name is Tulip, and I'm not a rock. Or an onion," she said, although she was unsure of the meaning of those two words. "I'm a tulip."

"I've never heard of a tulip, and I've been around for years," replied one of the roses. "Are you sure you're not an onion?"

"I'm sure," replied Tulip, disliking onions more and more every minute.

"Well you're certainly not showy, are you, dear?" asked Mrs. Popple, stretching her yellow petals and shaking her leaves. "I don't know of many flowers who live underground like that, but to each her own."

Tulip wasn't sure about her new companions, but since she was going to be there for a while she figured she'd better find a way to get along with them.

"Well, what should I look like? I don't think that the woman would have bought me if she didn't like the way I looked. There must be something appealing about me," said Tulip, thinking that this was the most obvious thing in the world.

"Well, sweetie, you never know with the woman," said Annabelle. "She might've felt sorry for you, since you're an onion and all." With a sigh, she smoothed her white petals and flicked a grasshopper off of her leaves.

And this was how the first few weeks of Tulip's life in the garden went. Annabelle and Mrs. Popple gave her counsel on how to be a better plant and could always be counted upon for unwanted advice. They assured her that she would be a lovely onion when she grew, and quite delicious at that; and they promised to never complain about how wretched she would smell. Then, at winter's arrival, the woman covered up the flowers to protect them from the harsh conditions, and Tulip didn't have to hear them speak anymore for a while.

During those cold months Tulip was still confined underground, but she befriended the heath who lived next to the flowerbed. Her name was Erica, and she didn't bloom until midwinter. Erica was happy to have company for the season.

"Why are you so lonely in the winter?" asked Tulip one day.

"Well, very few flowers are out in the cold months," replied Erica. "Usually everyone besides me is asleep at this time of year." She waved her white flowers so their intoxicating scent wafted through the hardened ground to Tulip, who loved to smell them.

"That must be terribly boring for you," said Tulip.

"At least I get to see things. You're missing so much, laying there in the dark all the time. I wish you could see everything up here with me. Spring and summer are nice; but to me, winter is the most beautiful season. Everything's so grey and peaceful. It's easier to enjoy things without those show-offs around." Erica said, gesturing to the sleeping daisies and other flowers.

As winter ended, it was time for Erica to rest until her season came again, and soon the snowdrops and Canterbury Bells came into bloom. They were friendly to Tulip, and curious to know if she was ever going to come above ground. It wasn't long before Tulip felt a strange sensation in her head. And then, one glorious day, she felt sunlight for the first time. A shoot had finally grown above ground.

"Can you see me? Can you see me?" she asked excitedly. The snowdrops cheered, and the daisies, who were just starting to wake up again, wondered what all the fuss was about. They had been snoozing beneath their covering for the whole of winter, and did not appreciate the disturbance.

Annabelle yawned. "Oh, is the onion still here?" she asked, wiping dew from her leaves.

"Yes, is she?" said Mrs. Popple. "I do hope so. I've had all winter to think of some more pointers to give you, dear. I know how much you need our advice."

The days passed, and Tulip grew taller and taller. The rest of the flowers grew too; the daffodils bloomed and the rosebushes put out tender little buds. Tulip noticed her head felt unusually heavy, and when she opened her eyes she was astonished. She could see again! The garden lay before her in its entirety. She saw Erica sleeping, and realized that Annabelle and Mrs. Popple really were as beautiful as they made themselves sound. The whole business was so overwhelming she almost wished she was still underground. Then the woman came out of the house.

"Well, well, well! The tulip has bloomed, and what a beauty she is!" The woman bent over and admired Tulip, who was indeed quite lovely. The woman's family joined her, and each person oohed and aahed over Tulip's flower.

"She's so pretty!" said one lady. "What a lovely color."

"Yes, see how purple she is! Absolutely gorgeous, and well worth the wait." The woman beamed proudly at Tulip, who was overjoyed with pleasure.

The daisies stood up straight and tall, showing each petal to its full potential, but all eyes were on Tulip, who was by far the main attraction of the garden. After that, she never again felt ashamed for being who she was, and held her head up high every day. As the years passed and new bulbs and other flowers were brought to the garden, she encouraged them to grow and made new friends. No flower was ever made to feel unwelcome in the garden again.

The Oak Tree Prince

Once upon a time, in a kingdom not too far from here, there was a king and queen who lived in a large and beautiful castle with their son. His name was Prince Daniel and he was not at all pleasant. As a young boy he had often amused himself with activities such as shooting spit-balls at ambassadors from other countries or throwing stones at the cats that lived in the gardens. When he grew up he took to cavorting around the country, spending his parents' money and refusing to study for his classes at the university. He chose instead to simply tell the professors that if they did not give him a satisfactory grade for the course, he would send them to live in the sewers. Needless to say, he always made excellent marks.

By the time Prince Daniel had reached marriageable age, he still had not chosen a wife and didn't seem at all intent on doing so. He would have had no trouble finding a girl to marry if it weren't for his extraordinarily haughty nature. He was a strong and intelligent young man, though he was more likely to use his brains to think of something nasty to say than for good.

One warm afternoon in late summer, Prince Daniel was lazing about outside the castle door, looking for something to provide him with entertainment. He knew his parents were inside at that moment trying to arrange an audience with some baroness or princess or something like that, but he really didn't care. Such negotiations took months to work out, and even then they were likely to fall flat. Odds were, he'd have lots of time in the coming years to have fun on his own. The thought made him giddy with happiness.

A few minutes later he saw an old sorcerer slowly approaching the castle door. Now, this was not a cruel, wicked sorcerer like those typically found in stories such as this. As a general rule he used his magical abilities to provide assistance to those in need, and to establish peace throughout the kingdom.

On this particular day, the sorcerer was coming to the castle for his weekly afternoon tea with the king. As the sorcerer raised his hand to lift the heavy brass knocker, Prince Daniel jumped out from the shadows and planted himself in front of the door.

"Just where do you think you're going?" Prince Daniel asked rudely, crossing his arms.

The sorcerer, in spite of his cordial nature, was in no mood to be trifled with. He had spent his entire morning on a house call sorting out a ridiculous argument between two girls and their stepsister (over a shoe, of all things). He had missed his lunch and was now very hungry and becoming increasingly crotchety with each wasted second.

"I'm here to have tea with your father, as I've done every Tuesday afternoon for the past thirty years," he answered. He was all too familiar with Prince Daniel's antics, and his stomach began to growl for want of watercress and smoked salmon sandwiches. "May I pass?" he asked, almost mockingly.

Prince Daniel didn't move. A charming, arrogant smile spread across his face.

"And why should I let you, old man? What have you done for me?"

There was a pause, during which the sorcerer's hunger evaporated and a smoldering flicker of anger filled his stomach instead. *Old man?* This little brat had the nerve to call him an *old man?* At four hundred and eighty-six years of age, he was certainly not an old man. No, he was quite young for a sorcerer; so young that he had only just begun to be taken seriously by his peers. Why, his mentor was nearing his nine hundredth birthday. (It was the next week, actually. The sorcerer made a mental note to buy a birthday present later that afternoon.)

Shaking his head furiously, the sorcerer pounded his staff upon the ground. No, no, this would not do. Nobody called him an *old man* and got away with it; least of all a spoiled, rotten, irresponsible prince.

Before Prince Daniel could say anything else, the sorcerer raised his staff. He muttered a few well-chosen words, and after a loud BANG and a blinding white light, the prince was gone. In his place next to the castle door stood a large, mature oak tree. Its leaves were bright green in the summer sunshine, and the bark was a beautiful grey color marked with knots and cracks.

The sorcerer looked up at the tree and smiled.

"Now, I haven't performed this spell in while, so I want to make sure I do this right, you know," he said, digging through his pockets for a moment before producing a battered leather-bound book. He slid his reading glasses into place and then flipped through the book until he came to the page he was looking for. He studied it carefully, nodding and murmuring all the while. Satisfied, he pocketed the book and called up to the oak tree that was once Prince Daniel.

"Normally, the statute of limitations for this spell is that a lady has to find your life worthy of saving before you become human again, but I think that some extra time in this…condition…would do you good," he said, laughing. "I believe that requiring a lady to save your life three times would be more appropriate."

The sorcerer then proceeded to forge a note from Prince Daniel, informing the king and queen that he had decided to ship off to Europe for a Grand Tour, where he would fill his head with all sorts of useful things. The sorcerer left the note on a table in the foyer and then had his tea with the king, just like normal.

Prince Daniel, needless to say, was not at all pleased with this. He tried shouting for the sorcerer to come back and turn him into a human again, but he couldn't speak. He tried to walk away, but all he could do was lift his roots a few inches above the ground. In fact, the only movement he could easily make was to wave his branches about where his arms had once been. Irritated by his newly restricted mobility, Prince Daniel tried to think of a way out of his predicament.

A lady had to save his life *three times* before he'd become human again? That seemed highly improbable, since Prince Daniel didn't know any ladies who really liked him, much less any who would be willing to save his life as a tree. He fumed bitterly and racked his brains to find a loophole in the spell, but did not succeed.

Inside, the sorcerer and the king were finishing up their tea when the queen entered the hall jubilantly, carrying "Daniel's" note. Once the king had read it, he and the queen immediately called to place an advertisement in the kingdom's newspaper stating that the castle would need a trustworthy caretaker (with references, of course) while they took a year-long Mediterranean cruise. When the tea was over and the sorcerer departed the castle, he waved merrily to the oak tree, which shook its branches angrily in response.

The next day, the king's and queen's advertisement was answered almost instantly by a young princess named Emmeline. With her grave face and thoughtful nature, Emmeline was known for her kindness and wisdom. None of which interested Daniel. In fact, when she moved her things into the castle, Prince Daniel was so unimpressed that he hardly even glanced at her.

The king and queen were quite eager for their trip, to put it mildly. They had married young after only being engaged for twenty-four hours—it was the custom in their day for a prince to propose marriage after simply deciding a princess was attractive—and they hadn't spent much time together before Daniel was born. They gave Emmeline a few last hurried instructions before dashing out the door to the carriage waiting for them. So hasty was their departure that the king and queen didn't even notice the grand oak tree's presence.

After seeing them off, Emmeline looked at the oak tree curiously before disappearing inside the castle. Prince Daniel scrutinized her appearance long after she left. She was dressed too plainly to be a proper princess, that was certain. Her face didn't appear very remarkable; in fact, he thought she looked downright boring. He dismissed her from his thoughts as darkness fell.

Emmeline introduced herself to the servants of the castle and made herself at home. She was both nervous and a little excited about living somewhere new, though her eagerness to flex her independence surpassed her fears. The castle seemed like a pleasant place, and she was particularly intrigued by the oak tree next to the door, the one whose leaves moved without the wind.

Summer carried on and spilled forth into autumn. Prince Daniel's once bright green leaves responded to the change by turning a brilliant, fiery red, much to his displeasure. He had expected the sorcerer to come groveling and turn him back into a human weeks ago; this "learning his lesson" business was taking far too long for his liking.

Emmeline took advantage of the fine weather by spending nearly every day outside, working in the garden with the servants or hanging linens out to dry. Prince Daniel could not understand why she was doing this. She was a *princess*, for crying out loud, so why was she outside doing servants' work? But what puzzled him more than anything was how happy she looked while participating in these tasks. Prince Daniel could think of nothing he would enjoy less than hanging linens, and pondered this every time he saw Emmeline laughing with the maids.

One crisp afternoon, the smell of baked apples filled the air as a teenage boy and girl from the nearby village approached the castle. The boy had come to ask Princess Emmeline if she was interested in purchasing his father's largest ram, and had brought his sweetheart along. Before knocking on the door, however, he turned and looked at the oak tree that was Prince Daniel.

"What a magnificent tree!" he told his sweetheart, who agreed heartily.

Prince Daniel straightened to his fullest height. *Yes, I am magnificent*, he thought to himself with pride.

But then the boy removed a pocketknife from his coat and walked toward the tree, saying, "Imagine how splendid our initials will look, carved into its bark." His voice was eager, and he raised the knife's blade with purpose.

Prince Daniel's sap ran cold and all proud thoughts vanished from his head. Surely this beastly child wasn't going to cut into him. He panicked, trying to think of a way to stop this before he was seriously injured. But the boy continued forward and placed the knife against the bark of the tree. Prince Daniel felt the blade's pressure, and his leaves shuddered from the cold touch.

Just as Prince Daniel steeled himself for the pain of the knife, the castle door opened and Princess Emmeline's voice rang out.

"What are you doing to that tree?"

The boy lowered his hand and turned scarlet in the face. Realizing what he had planned to do, Emmeline walked over to the boy and girl and explained kindly, "You really mustn't carve letters into the bark of a tree. Doing so could let all sorts of parasites into its wood, and it could get very sick and die."

"We're so sorry, Your Highness," the girl whispered. "We didn't know."

Emmeline sighed. "That's all right, just don't let it happen again. I don't think there was any harm done. It would be a shame, since I do believe this is a special tree," she said, placing her hand on the trunk where the boy had been about to carve. Prince Daniel was surprised at how warm and soft her hand was. Princess Emmeline did buy the boy's biggest ram, which was brought to the castle promptly, and Prince Daniel's bark was indeed unharmed; though the incident had greatly unsettled him. For the first time, he was truly thankful for Emmeline's presence.

And so Prince Daniel's life was saved once.

Winter fell across the kingdom, bringing with it a blanket of snow. The unfortunate change in weather made Prince Daniel irritable and grouchy since he was used to spending his winters warming himself by the castle fires and eating delicious hot food. But his spirits rose one afternoon as Emmeline came outside, carrying a large sack in her arms. She set it down in front of the oak tree and opened it, removing several round bird puddings to hang upon the tree.

How considerate of her, Prince Daniel thought once he understood that Princess Emmeline had made the puddings out of seeds and suet in order to feed the hungry birds. It became clear at once that Emmeline couldn't possibly reach high enough to hang the puddings, so Prince Daniel lowered a branch for her, much to her delight.

"How brilliant!" she cried. "I always knew there was something special about you! What a wonderful tree you are."

Happy to indulge her, Prince Daniel lowered more branches. She darted about, hanging more and more puddings until there was none left and the tree was full.

With one last look at her handiwork, Emmeline went back inside.

I am a wonderful tree, Prince Daniel thought to himself, and then realized he actually wasn't the least bit wonderful. In fact, he was rather dreadful to be around as a human. Contemplating this, Prince Daniel came to the awful conclusion that if Emmeline had known him before he became a tree she would've found him horrible. And, sadly, she would be quite right.

Many birds came and alighted on his branches to enjoy the meal Emmeline had left for them. At first, Prince Daniel made to shake them off as he had always done, but, remembering Emmeline's compassion, chose not to. He was surprised to find that he liked the birds very much, and their sweet songs made him cheerful in the midst of the dismal snow.

Now, there was a man named Lord Charles who had heard of a wise princess named Emmeline, and decided he would seek her as his wife. Lord Charles was a charismatic man, known for his ambition and smooth words. But he was also deceptive and cruel at times, taking care only to advance his own political interests. A union with Emmeline would be a strategic one, in his mind. It would do well to have a wife known more for her brains than her beauty.

So Lord Charles set out for the kingdom in early spring. The countryside was overflowing with daffodils, lavender, and primroses, but he took no notice. He was in a great hurry to win his wife and start campaigning against other kingdoms, and flowers would only slow him down. When he finally arrived, Lord Charles booked at room at the village inn before heading to the castle, so as not to appear too expectant.

The harsh winter weather had kept Princess Emmeline indoors for long periods of time, and Prince Daniel found that he missed seeing her. He had used his time of solitude to reflect on his character, and found himself thinking of ways to improve. He hoped that if he was ever restored to human form, Emmeline would consider him worthy of her.

One warm afternoon, Prince Daniel was waiting quietly to see if Emmeline would come out to sit under the shade of his branches when he saw the proud, calculating form of Lord Charles approaching the castle. As the visitor stepped up to the castle door, Prince Daniel heard him muttering to himself.

"This shouldn't be difficult," Lord Charles was saying. "She probably doesn't have many suitors calling, so it's likely that she'll be desperate for some attention. We'll be married within the month, I'd say, and I shall probably receive fifty thousand acres—at the least—as a gift from her father. What a fine addition of land that will be!"

And after smoothing his hair, he raised the brass knocker and rapped it three times against the door.

Prince Daniel was not at all pleased with this. He had grown rather fond of Emmeline over the past several months, and did not approve of this Lord Charles character speaking of her in such a way. He longed more than anything to reach out with his branches and strangle the charlatan, but thought it might be an unwise choice. He settled instead on allowing his leaves to shake violently. Lord Charles looked up at the oak tree with a confused expression on his face, but smiled pleasantly when the castle door opened to reveal Emmeline.

"May I help you?" she asked.

Lord Charles answered, "Madam, my name is Lord Charles, and I have heard tell of a princess who is wiser and lovelier than any other princess in the world. I see now that you are certainly she." He gave her another winning smile. "You are Princess Emmeline, correct?"

Emmeline's expression remained thoughtful, for she was not taken in by Lord Charles's thick flattery. Prince Daniel was glad of this. Emmeline took a moment to regard the suitor before answering.

"Yes, my lord, I am Emmeline. The lady of this house," she said graciously. "You must have come a long way; may I offer you some refreshment?"

Lord Charles's grin became wider, if that were possible. "I humbly thank you, Your Highness. You are too generous." He followed her inside, and the door closed heavily behind him.

Prince Daniel strained to hear the conversation taking place in the castle, but to no avail. Instead he was left to his own thoughts as the afternoon progressed. It wasn't until the sun was beginning to set that the castle door finally opened and Lord Charles stepped over the threshold into the evening air.

"I thank you once again for your hospitality, Princess Emmeline," he said. "I had a lovely time with you." He bowed deeply, and Prince Daniel thought he saw Emmeline roll her eyes. But Lord Charles was not finished yet. "I wonder, Your Highness, if it would be too much trouble for me to return tomorrow evening and enjoy more of your company?"

Absolutely not, Prince Daniel thought to himself, trying desperately to think of some way to deter Lord Charles. Then an idea occurred to him. Before Emmeline could answer, Prince Daniel shook his branches so fiercely that dozens of large, hard acorns rained down upon Lord Charles, who flung his hands over his head angrily.

Emmeline burst into laughter, which only added fuel to Lord Charles's fury. Cheered by Emmeline's response, Prince Daniel lifted one of his roots and wrapped it around Lord Charles's left ankle, causing him to stumble.

Lord Charles looked so ridiculous hopping around and trying to regain his balance that Emmeline couldn't help but laugh more. Utterly embarrassed, and not one to tolerate humor at his expense, Lord Charles lost his patience. He glared at the tree.

"This tree is evil, Your Highness! You should have it removed from the grounds at once. Do you not see the way it is humiliating me?"

Emmeline's laughter died away, and her face became quite serious. "Lord Charles," she said coolly, "I happen to like that tree very much. It is certainly not evil; it is anything but, and I'll thank you not to shout at me so."

Lord Charles's shame increased and, breathing loudly through his nose, he turned and trudged back toward the village.

Princess Emmeline waited until he was well out of earshot before she started laughing again. The image of the oak tree's acorns raining down like hailstones upon him was too funny for her to contain, and she looked at the oak tree happily.

"He was dreadful," she said to no one in particular. "I don't think he asked me a single question about myself all evening."

After she went inside to bed, Prince Daniel swayed his branches joyfully for quite a while, so relieved was he by Emmeline's assessment of Lord Charles.

But Lord Charles was still very angry that the tree had humiliated him. In his mind, the interfering oak had not only cost him his pride, but possibly fifty thousand acres and a tactical marriage as well. When he got back to the inn, he decided to wait until after midnight and then light a torch and head back to the castle so he might exact his revenge. Emmeline's affections for the tree meant absolutely nothing to him; he had every intention of watching that wretched oak burn.

Emmeline had not been asleep for very long when a maid came to her room and alerted her that someone was approaching the castle. Pulling on a dressing gown, Emmeline rushed to the window where she recognized the shape of Lord Charles, carrying a torch. She suspected what he was up to, and instructed one of the maids to bring her a pail of water once she was outside.

Prince Daniel had seen Lord Charles coming toward him with the threatening weapon, but he wasn't the least bit afraid. In fact, he was more worried about Emmeline and what would happen to her once he had burned up. He despised Lord Charles and decided he wasn't going to give in without a fight. Readying his branches, Prince Daniel prepared to ward off Lord Charles's torch.

Lord Charles had nearly reached Prince Daniel when the castle doors burst open and Emmeline strode outside into the darkness.

"Stop this at once, sir," she said firmly. Her maid brought the pail of water she had requested. Emmeline took it, walked over to the tree, and stood facing Lord Charles. "I am asking you now to leave—a request you will only receive once."

But Lord Charles just brandished the torch danger-
ously close to Prince Daniel, shouting, "There is some
sort of evil spirit living in this tree! I am doing you a
favor, Your Highness, by getting rid of it for you!"

Angry and afraid for Emmeline, Prince Daniel raised
his branches high as Lord Charles reached out with his
torch to set them ablaze.

But he never got the chance. Princess Emmeline
threw the contents of the pail onto the torch, ex-
tinguishing it, and succeeded in soaking Lord Charles
rather thoroughly as well. Furious, Lord Charles hurled
the useless torch to the ground, but Emmeline didn't
back away.

"I will not have you damage this property, Lord
Charles," she said. "As I told you before: I am the lady
of the house, and I am ordering you to leave." She
pointed toward the village. "I do not wish to see you
ever again."

Lord Charles looked as if he wanted to object, but
when he saw all of the servants and maids looking
furiously at him from the castle windows he picked up
the ruined torch and retreated to the village.

Prince Daniel felt his heart swell with affection for
Emmeline, and even after she had gone back inside the

castle, he found himself unable to sleep. He could not stop thinking about her bravery and compassion toward him: a simple tree.

And so Prince Daniel's life was saved twice.

The spring melted into summer, and it would soon be time for Princess Emmeline to leave. The king and queen would be returning from their cruise in a few weeks, and Prince Daniel's heart grew heavy at the thought. He did not know if he would ever become human again, but if Emmeline wasn't going to be at the castle anymore, he didn't care. He had changed so much in the past year because of her, and he was going to miss her dearly when she left. Thankfully, Emmeline spent a large part of each day sitting with her back against his trunk, reading or resting, and he took great pleasure in shading her from the sun with his branches. But more than anything he wished simply for his arms to return, so that with them he might hold her.

On the afternoon before the king's and queen's expected return, Emmeline was reclining in the shade of the oak tree, also wishing she didn't have to leave. She had grown rather attached to the castle and its mysterious oak that moved when there was no wind. It had been a delightful year and she wasn't sure what she was going to do when she left. She would have to figure something out, and soon.

But before she had much more time to think about her future, a large man bearing an axe strolled toward the castle door, whistling. When he saw Emmeline, he removed his hat and bowed.

"Your Highness, I have orders from the Society of Home Safety to have this tree removed from your property," he said, gesturing to Prince Daniel with a sheet of paper.

Emmeline stood up, took the paper, and examined it. Indeed, it was a letter from the Society of Home Safety stating that the tree posed a danger to the castle's foundation and must be removed immediately. There was a list of several signatures and an official looking seal at the bottom of the page.

Confused, Emmeline looked at the man. "What is the Society of Home Safety? I've never even heard of it before."

The man shrugged, but in truth he knew that there was no Society of Home Safety. This was a scheme thought of by Lord Charles as a last attempt to get rid of the dangerous, evil oak tree. Desperate to have

Emmeline for his wife, he had invented the bogus organization, forged the signatures, and paid the axe man to carry out the deed.

"But, sir," she started, "I don't understand—"

"I'll need that letter back, Your Highness."

Stunned into silence, Emmeline returned the letter to the man, who shouldered his axe once more and approached the tree. Prince Daniel gave an involuntary shudder. He could not see a way out of this, but simply looked sadly at Emmeline, who was growing anxious.

"Please, please, there must be something I can do," she argued. "There's nothing wrong with this tree. It's not damaging the castle at all, I'm sure."

But the man wasn't listening. He was busy examining the tree, deciding where to strike. "I've got the signatures, Your Highness. The tree has to go." He frowned as he looked at her distressed face. "If you don't mind my asking, why do you care so much, anyway?"

Emmeline wrung her hands as tears filled her eyes. "I don't know! It's just…I know that it's special. There's something different about this tree, and you mustn't cut it down!" she cried despairingly, all composure gone.

The man shrugged again, and made to raise his axe. Prince Daniel's love for Emmeline filled his heart as he faced the axe, which would surely bring his death. Praying that Emmeline would find the true love and happiness that she deserved, he awaited the axe's blow.

The man lifted the axe over his head and prepared to swing. Suddenly sure of what she needed to do, Emmeline seized the axe's handle right beneath its head and pulled backwards with all her might. Surprised, the man released the axe, which fell with Emmeline and landed on the ground beside her.

"Enough of this, Your Highness," the man said irritably as tears streamed down Emmeline's face. He reached to pick up the axe, but when he turned around he saw an amazing sight. The tree was shrinking, its branches and roots retracting into itself; and almost instantly, a humbler, kinder Prince Daniel stood before Emmeline, restored to his human form. Once again, the axe hit the ground with a thud as its owner gaped at the spectacle, unable to believe his eyes.

Emmeline was still sitting where she had fallen, though by now her tears had stopped and she was quite terrified. Convinced she was dreaming, she didn't move as Prince Daniel came over to her and knelt, taking her hand in his.

"My beloved Princess Emmeline," he said to her, "my name is Daniel, and it was nearly a year ago that I was a terrible, selfish prince that a sorcerer turned into a tree. He told me that until a lady saved my life three times, I would never become human again. You have indeed saved my life three times, but you have also done much more than that. You showed me how to be compassionate, brave, and loyal as well. I can tell you honestly that I am not the same person I was before I became a tree, and I would like to say now that I love you with all of my heart."

He paused, unsure whether to continue since Emmeline was still staring at him with a frozen expression in her eyes. "I-I should very much like to kiss you, if that is all right," he said, turning rather red in the face.

Emmeline looked at him for a moment, trying to make sense of how this young man could have both the appearance of a stranger and the air of a steadfast companion. Not just a companion, but a friend with whom she had shared many peculiar and wonderful experiences over the past twelve months.

"You were that tree all this time?" she finally asked with a shaking voice. "The tree that helped me feed the birds in the winter and shaded me in the summer? The tree that made Lord Charles so angry and moved without the wind?" She pointed to the spot next to the castle door where he had stood as the oak.

Prince Daniel nodded solemnly, and Emmeline wiped a single tear from her cheek as she smiled at him.

"All right, you may kiss me."

And so, as endings often go in these stories, all was well.

Sir Andrew and Sophia

Long ago there lived a very old king who had no heir. He was a wise king, and knew that upon his death many of his rivals would attempt to seize his kingdom by force if he did not choose someone to succeed him. Only a good, noble leader would do; one who possessed true valor and kindness. In order to find this person, the king met with his council and devised a series of challenges so great that only the boldest would attempt them. The one who successfully overcame the obstacles and reached the castle would be named heir to the throne.

Knights and nobles came from far and near to try for the king's throne, each more brave and daring than the last. They lined up outside the heavy iron gates, anxious for their chance. They talked eagerly as they waited, comparing their weapons and armor and titles.

One knight, by the name of Sir Andrew, did not participate in the sporting jests. He was a poor knight and had traveled a great distance for this opportunity. His armor was streaked with rust, his sword's blade needed to be sharpened, and his old horse flicked her tangled tail at the flies buzzing around her mud-splashed flanks. The other knights and nobles smirked when they saw him.

"What are you doing here?" they called from their gleaming mounts. "You know nothing of courage or chivalry or honor. Give up your place so that a worthier fighter may have a chance."

Sir Andrew ignored them. For two days he waited, moving slowly forward in the line, until at last he reached the gates. With a gust of wind, the gates blew open, revealing a dark forest. The wind drew Sir Andrew and his horse into the darkness, and then slammed the gates shut behind them.

Sir Andrew looked around, though there was not much to see. Tall trees rose in every direction, their thick branches blotting out any trace of sunlight hoping to reach the forest floor. The dank smell of moss filled

Sir Andrew's nostrils. His horse whinnied and took a hesitant step forward. Then Sir Andrew heard a voice.

"Dismount, brave knight, before you proceed. For only the most sure-footed are fit to reign."

Sir Andrew obeyed, leaving his faithful mare behind. He drew his sword and set forth. His progress was slow; the darkness seemed to intensify with each step he took. Within moments he could not even see the narrow path before his feet. He stopped, unsure where to go, when a bright spot of light caught his eye. He made his way to it, stepping carefully to avoid any nasty creatures lurking in the undergrowth. As he came closer he saw the source of the light was a small oil lamp held by a young woman.

"I beg your pardon, madam," said the knight, with a stiff bow. "My name is Sir Andrew. As you see, it's quite dark in these woods, and I wanted to know if I might trouble you for your light."

The young woman smiled. "I know who you are, Sir Andrew," she said. "I am Sophia. If the light is your desire you may have it, but only if you are willing to bring me along on your journey."

Sir Andrew agreed, and the two set off together through the woods. Sophia's small lamp cast just enough light to illuminate a few feet of the path at a time. Occasionally, they heard shrill cries and snarls from the dark woods, but they continued forward. Sir Andrew followed close behind Sophia, grateful for the lamp. When he told her this, she laughed.

"I am glad to hear you say it," she replied. "But you should know, Sir Andrew, that you are the first to accept my offer."

"You mean none of the others wanted your light?"

She shrugged. "They would rather find their way on their own," she said.

Sir Andrew thought this was foolish, as you probably do, but he said nothing else about it, for he was distracted by a sudden movement in the trees. He stopped.

"Did you see that?" he said to Sophia. "I think I saw someone behind that tree."

Sophia turned to him. "There are many deceitful spirits in these woods," she said. "They'll show you beautiful things, but they can only make false promises. If you allow them to draw you off the path you'll be lost forever."

The trees became still again, and the two continued. For some time there was no other sound but their own footsteps. Sir Andrew grew tired of the monotonous journey, and his eyes drifted from the path once more. But instead of dark trees he saw a great sprawling castle, inviting and brightly lit.

He stopped walking, entranced by the lovely picture. It changed, and he now saw himself dressed in fine armor and riding a charger so large and powerful his enemies cowered at the sight of it. He saw himself dancing with princesses more beautiful than angels, their eyes alight with laughter. He reached out his hand, hoping to run his fingers through their gleaming hair. The princesses smiled shyly and beckoned for him to join them. Sir Andrew nodded, ready to oblige, when he heard Sophia's voice.

"Sir Andrew!" she called. "What are you doing?"

Silence filled the woods. The merry tableau had vanished, replaced by the sinister trees once more. Sir Andrew looked down and realized that without knowing it, he had turned away from Sophia and lifted one foot to step off the path. He lowered his foot sheepishly and did not waver from the path again.

Soon the forest came to an end. Sir Andrew squinted in the bright sunlight and saw a castle in the distance. But surrounding the castle was a marsh, stretching in every direction. Frightful creatures with sharp teeth and vicious tempers swam through the murky water, threatening to devour anyone who lost their footing. Before they could set out, however, Sir Andrew heard a voice.

"Remove your armor, bold knight, for a true leader leaves himself vulnerable to pain and suffering for the sake of his people."

Sir Andrew removed his armor one piece at a time and left it in a pile near the edge of the marsh, tying his sword belt around his waist. Sophia, still holding her lamp, led the way into the maze of scrubby brown grass. Apart from the occasional splash, everything was quiet. Their progress was slow, and much to Sir Andrew's consternation they seemed to be moving away from the castle instead of toward it. He suggested trying a different route, but Sophia shook her head.

"Don't let your eyes fool you," she told him. "The shortest route is not always the best."

Sir Andrew did not want to agree, but then he remembered the mistake he had almost made in the forest. He followed behind Sophia, amazed at her ability to navigate the tricky path. Everything was going well until, suddenly, Sophia slipped. A terrible squid wrapped one of its white tentacles tightly around her ankle, pulling her foot down toward the dark water. Sir

Andrew rushed forward and caught her before she fell, and with one swift movement pulled his sword from its sheath and cut through the white tentacle, freeing Sophia's leg.

"Are you all right?" he asked her, as the squid disappeared with a small splash.

"I am," said Sophia. She examined her lamp to make sure the wick wasn't damaged. "Thank you, Sir Andrew. You are quite the agile knight."

Sir Andrew dried his sword on the grass and they continued on their way. He stayed close to Sophia and kept a watchful eye out for any other unseemly creatures that might cause her harm. At long last they arrived at the castle door.

"Leave your sword, valiant knight," said the voice, "for the greatest kings are those who rely on wisdom and faith to be his guides."

Sir Andrew placed his sword on the ground and looked anxiously toward the door. His uncertainty increased when Sophia smiled at him and said, "This is where we part ways." She planted a kiss on his cheek. "Godspeed, Sir Andrew."

Poor Sir Andrew felt terribly alone as he passed through the castle door. He found himself in a small chamber, its stone walls hung with rich, colorful tapestries. Before him stood a wooden table, and on that table sat three items. The first was a sword, sleek and intimidating and fitted with a blade sharper than any razor. The second was a golden crown set with glittering diamonds and emeralds as large as eggs. The last item was a simple hammer. Its head was scratched and dull, and its handle was caked with mud. As Sir Andrew studied the items, he heard the voice once more.

"Choose wisely, gallant knight, which instrument you shall use to rule."

Carefully, Sir Andrew considered each item. The sword, while menacing, might be chosen by someone who would rule with force, imposing his power on his own people. The crown might attract a man who merely desired the position of king and all the glory and adulation that came with such a title. The hammer, however, was just a humble tool. It could be used to build and create as well as administer justice and provide protection when necessary.

Sir Andrew made his choice. With a deep breath, he picked up the hammer and passed through the door. What he saw nearly made him drop the hammer in alarm. He was in a great hall filled with hundreds of people; the sound of their cheers reached the rafters high above them. To his surprise, he saw Sophia making her way to him through the throng, dressed in fine clothes and smiling radiantly. She took his hand and led him to an elderly man seated in a throne.

"Sir Andrew," said Sophia, "I'd like you to meet the king."

The old king greeted him warmly and declared Sir Andrew the heir to his kingdom. Sir Andrew married Sophia, and they reigned together with great wisdom and joy for many years.

The Ice Garden

In a country not too far from here there stood a great house, larger than any you've ever seen. It was filled with more rooms than you could count in a day and portraits of grandly dressed men and women hung from nearly every wall. The kitchens always smelled of good things to eat and the grounds were filled with beautiful parks and gardens and a heated pond with a tiny island in the center. In nearly every garden there stood a statue, and one of these depicted a young shepherd carved from stone, with two stone dogs alert at his side.

Unlike the other statues who enjoyed the sweet fragrance of spring, the long days of summer, and the blazing colors of autumn, the shepherd enjoyed winter best of all. The man and woman who lived in the house loved to host parties out of doors, no matter the season. So when the cold settled in they ordered the finest ice sculptures to serve as special decorations. The grounds were studded with men and women, boys and girls, and animals of every type, all carved from ice. If you were to look down from the uppermost windows in the house on a sunny day, it would look as though the house were surrounded by a maze of glittering creatures.

One night after such a party, when all the guests had gone to bed, the shepherd decided to walk through the grounds and meet the newcomers. Some of the other statues tried to discourage him.

"Those ice sculptures are all snobs," said a granite girl holding a violin. "They'll never speak to you."

A marble goddess tossed her hair. "They think they're so beautiful. As if there's anything remotely lovely about frozen water."

The little bronze centaur propping open the garden gate shouted in agreement from his platform: "I'd crush them into snow if I could. Every last one!"

The shepherd did not listen. He whistled for his dogs, took up his staff, and started off. He soon came across an icy knight with frosted armor, but when the shepherd raised his hand in greeting the knight slammed his visor shut and abruptly turned away. Next, the shepherd approached a group of young women playing musical instruments. From the smiles on their faces he thought they might be pleased at his company, but then the girl sitting behind the glassy harp turned to the singer beside her and commented in a poorly concealed whisper on the shepherd's weathered face and hands. Nasty giggles spread through the circle and, embarrassed, the shepherd bade them farewell. Even the frozen geese, soaring through the air, looked down at him disdainfully.

Defeated, the shepherd turned his gaze back toward the gardens. Perhaps the statues were right after all. He looked down at his cracked stone hands and wondered how anyone—ice or stone—could find them worthy. But he did not have long to feel sorry for himself. A terrible roar sounded from the bushes and a gleaming ice tiger shot out of the shadows, running straight for his dogs. Without stopping to think, the shepherd raised his staff and charged toward the tiger. He braced himself for the beast's sharp teeth and claws, but stopped when a bright light flashed before his eyes. He looked up to see the tiger swatting at the light, which was not actually a light at all, but an icy falcon with moonlight reflecting off its wings. The falcon dove at the tiger again and again, always dodging the tiger's claws. The tiger eventually grew so frustrated it gave an annoyed roar and slunk back into the bushes, leaving the shepherd and his dogs unharmed.

The shepherd watched the falcon in amazement as it glided like a shooting star over the parks and toward the pond. He followed the bird at once, his dogs barking eagerly as they raced beside him. When he finally reached the edge of the pond he stood rooted to the ground, unable to tear his eyes away from the little island where the falcon alighted on the arm of a young woman carved perfectly from ice.

Never before had the shepherd seen such beauty. She was a huntress, with a bow in her hand and the falcon on her arm. A quiver full of icy arrows was slung across her back, and the folds of her dress draped softly around her knees. A wreath of flowers crowned her hair, and at the sight of her gentle eyes the shepherd's mouth became very dry. He bowed awkwardly and tried to thank her for sending her falcon to save his dogs, but he could not form the words. The huntress smiled shyly in reply, but then she did an alarming thing. She pulled an arrow from her quiver and fitted it to her bow. The falcon hovered overhead as she drew the string and, to the shepherd's horror, aimed the arrow at him. The shepherd swallowed and took a step back. Perhaps he was wrong and the other statues were right. Even the bravest and loveliest ice sculptures were all terrible snobs and wanted nothing to do with a weathered stone shepherd.

But then the huntress tilted her bow upward and loosed the arrow high into the sky. It soared high in a great arc across the water, and then landed at the shepherd's feet. He pulled it out of the ground and grinned from ear to ear. There, twined around the arrow's shaft, was an ice rose, as clear and pure as crystal.

Every night afterwards, the shepherd visited the pond. The huntress sent him letters etched on thin sheets of ice and rolled into scrolls, which the falcon carried to him from the island. He carved his replies on stone tablets and sent them adrift on little rafts. But he wanted to speak with her face to face. Again and again he tried to find a way to reach the huntress. The owners of the house kept the pond heated, in case any of their guests wanted to go for a warm winter swim, making it impossible for the huntress to cross on her own. She'd melt as soon as she set one icy foot in the water. The shepherd, being made of stone, obviously could not swim. He'd sink to the muddy bottom and never been seen again.

First the shepherd tried to make a boat out of discarded planks bound together with honeysuckle vines. But when he set it in the pond the boards swelled and water seeped through the gaps. It capsized and broke apart into a dozen useless pieces. Next he tried to fashion a bridge out of rope so that the huntress might crawl out across over the water. This worked well at first; the cord was thick and held its shape stiffly so that it looked like a ladder. But there wasn't enough cord to reach the island. With each failed attempt the shepherd grew more frustrated. It didn't help that the other statues taunted him mercilessly.

"You're wasting your time," said a bust of Hermes, shaking his winged helmet at the shepherd. "You'll never reach the island."

"And even if you did," put in one of the muses, "what makes you think she'll want to come? I doubt she'd want to leave her precious little island. She's far too *important* to mingle with the other ice sculptures, much less you."

An old general astride his horse nodded gravely. "Mark my words," he warned. "You will regret this."

The shepherd paid them no mind. Later that night he paced the edge of the pond, wishing desperately for a way to reach the island. He absently picked up a pebble and tossed it into the water. To his horror, one of his dogs charged into the pond after the pebble. The shepherd shouted for his dog to stop before he sank, but the dog did not sink. The water scarcely reached his knees. He picked up the pebble in his jaws, trotted back through the shallow water, and dropped it at the shepherd's feet.

Amazed, the shepherd approached the dark blue water. He put his foot in and realized a smooth stone ledge ran beneath the surface of the lake. It didn't last long; after a few yards the ledge dropped off, but it still gave the shepherd an idea. If he couldn't build a bridge over the water, perhaps he could build a bridge from below. He dashed into the woods and sought out the largest boulders he could carry or roll to the pond and began piling them into the water. The job was a slow one, though over the next several nights his work drew him closer and closer to the island. The huntress waited patiently, sending her falcon to drop her roses and letters to the shepherd.

At last on one starry night, the bridge was ready. The shepherd laid his staff on the bank and ordered his dogs to stay. The narrow path of smooth stepping stones broke the surface of the water, glowing in the moonlight. Taking a deep breath, the shepherd stepped from one stone to the next until finally his sandaled foot touched the grassy island. There, standing before him, was the huntress. Up close she looked more beautiful than he ever imagined, and when she kissed his cheek with her icy lips his stone heart nearly stopped with delight. The falcon circled overhead as the shepherd lifted the huntress into his arms and carried her with great care back over the stepping stones. The other statues and ice sculptures watched them enter the gardens with open mouths, and the stars smiled down on them all night.

The next morning the lady of the house led her guests on a tour through the gardens. The sun beat down on them and more than one person removed their coat.

"I do love a warm winter day," said the lady. "It's so unexpected, like a little gift to remind us spring will arrive soon."

The ladies strolled along the brick paths and admired the statues. When they stopped before the stone shepherd and dogs one of the guests frowned. "Goodness," she said, "look at this one. I daresay I've never seen such a forlorn face on a statue."

The lady surveyed the shepherd. He did look different; instead of the strong, happy expression she remembered, his face was crumpled in agony. Even the dogs at his feet looked miserable, their ears and tails drooping listlessly.

"How curious," the lady said. "Well, let us continue. Be careful there, don't get your shoes wet."

The ladies stepped around a large puddle in front of the shepherd and left the garden. But if they had looked closely at the shepherd's hand, still shadowed by the garden wall and out of the bright sun, they would have seen him clutching all that was left of his huntress: a glistening ice rose.

The Water Child

A long time ago in a faraway kingdom there lived a king and queen. They were kind and just and showed great love for their subjects, but their happy lives lacked one thing: a child. The king brought in the finest doctors and physicians in all the land in hopes that they could help his wife. Finally, after several years of waiting and praying, the queen gave birth to a beautiful baby girl. She was named Nerine, which means "swimmer", for the kingdom contained many large, wonderful lakes, and the water played an integral part in all the subjects' lives. Every person in the kingdom rejoiced at the princess's birth.

Except for one. The queen's closest friend and most trusted advisor positively swelled with envy every time she saw the little princess. She was a sorceress, and though she possessed no royal blood she had been named successor to the throne in the event that the king and queen produced no heir. And now this horrible baby, with her soft skin and tiny hands, had ruined her carefully laid plans.

But the sorceress was not one to give up easily. One week after Nerine's birth a banquet was held in the new princess's honor. The baby could not be present during the whole feast due to its late hour, so as soon as the nurse left to take her to the nursery the sorceress excused herself and followed after her. She ordered the nurse to carry the baby down to the largest lake at the edge of the kingdom and throw her into the water. The nurse protested, but in the end she was so afraid of the sorceress that she agreed.

Nerine slept soundly in the nurse's arms, unaware of her unfortunate journey. The sky was clear that night, but the trees were so thick the nurse could scarcely see where she was going. She gripped the baby tightly, afraid she might trip and fall. When she reached the edge of the lake she looked down at Nerine's sleeping face. Tears filled her eyes and she sat on the bank, rocking the baby one last time.

"Such a sweet child," she cooed, wiping her eyes. "I wonder what kind of princess you would have made."

The nurse stalled as much as she dared, but she knew she would eventually have to do the deed. She stood up and prepared to carry out the sorceress's orders. But when she looked down, the baby's tiny mouth opened into a delicate yawn. The nurse froze. What was she thinking? She couldn't drown a baby. She debated several minutes over how she should proceed. In the end she decided the most prudent thing to do was leave the baby on the bank and hope a passing farmer or villager would hear her cries. Better to be raised a pauper, she thought, than to die a princess. She kissed the sleeping baby and laid the tiny bundle in the soft grass, then returned to the castle before she could change her mind.

Over the coming days a frantic search was led for the infant princess. The king and queen were beside themselves with shock and despair. They offered immeasurable sums of money to anyone who might find their daughter, but no one was able to provide any information. The days stretched into weeks, and the weeks into months before the search was finally called off. The sorceress silently congratulated herself when she saw black flags hanging from the castle spires, and dark swathes of mourning cloth covering nearly every surface. It seemed her road to the throne was clear once more and the Princess Nerine gone forever, never to return.

Seventeen years later a young girl stood at the edge of a frozen lake, stomping her feet to keep warm. The lake was so large she could just make out the trees lining the opposite edge, a thick frosting of snow hiding their evergreen boughs. The air smelled of ice and smoke from distant fires. The surface of the lake was quiet, frozen and gray. There was no gentle rippling or occasional splash from a fish testing the air. No birds chirped in the woods behind her; there was hardly a sound to be heard.

"Nerine, why are you sulking?" said a voice suddenly. "It's a beautiful day."

The breeze picked up, blowing the dusting of snow on the lake's surface into the shape of a woman. This was Meris, a water nymph. She and her two sisters lived in the great lake, maintaining order and balance between the water and living things in it. (Every lake has its own trio of nymphs. They are intelligent, proud creatures, and they are not very warm toward most humans. If you ever meet one I suggest you mind your manners. In fact, it's probably best to just excuse yourself politely and be on your way before you say something silly and accidentally offend them. A water nymph is not an enemy you want to make for yourself.)

"If you wish to swim I can make a little pool for you," continued Meris. "I can heat it so you feel like you're in a hot spring. Let Aunt Meris help."

Nerine sighed. She loved the nymphs, and she knew they loved her. They told her many times how they had found her as a baby and taken on the task of raising her as their own. But she was still lonely. She had grown up watching from a distance as boys and girls played and swam in the lake, never joining them because of her aunts' warnings about other humans. Now she was older, and she wanted some new companions besides the fish and turtles in the lake.

"I'm all right, Aunt Meris," said Nerine. She stood up and drew her coat tightly around her. "I think I'll just go for a walk."

Nerine wandered along the edge of the lake, shivering from the wind. Soon she heard the sound of distant laughter and saw several figures lacing up their skates and gliding onto the ice. One in particular caught her eye, a handsome boy with a wide smile. He moved across the ice with great athleticism and skill. Nerine ventured closer, trying not to stare at him outright. He noticed her and raised his hand in greeting, and she smiled sheepishly in return. He started to call out to her, but he never got the chance. At that moment he skated over a thin patch of ice, and with a loud and horrible crash disappeared into the freezing water below.

For a split second there was nothing but silence. Then everyone on the lake rushed over to the new hole, careful not to come too close lest they fall in as well. But there was no sign of the boy. Horrified, Nerine sprinted onto the ice, pushed through the throng, and dove into the water.

For anyone else this would have been a foolish and possibly fatal thing to do. But Nerine was not like anyone else. She had learned how to swim before she could walk, and though she did not love the lake in winter, the icy water did not affect her as it would you and I.

Nerine swam quickly through the murky lake, pushing the water aside with long, powerful strokes. The heavy ceiling of ice made it dark and nearly impossible to see, but Nerine soon spotted the boy sinking toward the depths of the lake. His eyes were closed and a stream of tiny bubbles flowed from his mouth. Nerine reached the boy before he disappeared into the endless forest of reeds and lifted him under his arms, swimming back toward the surface. But there was one problem: she had lost sight of the hole in the ice.

"What's the matter, sweetheart?" said a voice.

Nerine looked to her right and saw Meris hovering in the water beside her, a falsely sympathetic smile on her face. She shifted the boy in her arms, straining from the weight.

"You shouldn't have let him fall through the ice," replied Nerine. "You had no reason."

Meris shrugged. "He was showing off," she said. "I don't care for show-offs."

"Please, Aunt Meris," begged Nerine. "Please melt the ice."

Meris rolled her eyes, then reconsidered when she saw how much Nerine was struggling. Nerine could hold her breath much longer than an ordinary human, but with the weight of the boy tugging her downward and the amount of time she had been underwater, she was starting to fade. Reluctantly, Meris raised her hand and placed it on the underside of the ice. As the youngest of the nymphs she was responsible for the lake's temperature, and at her touch the ice thinned and melted away. A perfectly round hole opened up over Nerine's head, and with her very last bit of strength she thrust the boy out of the water and onto the ice.

The boy coughed and gasped for air. The others saw him and shouted, hysterical with concern. Nerine felt a hand on her arm. She looked down and saw Meris.

"He's fine now," said Meris. "Swim back home before anyone notices you."

Nerine nodded, though before she sank back into the water she looked at the boy one more time. He was staring at her, shivering and wiping water from his eyes.

"Thank you," he said in a quiet, shaky voice. "Who are you?"

Nerine did not have a chance to answer, for the crowd had nearly reached the hole. She took a deep breath and dove underwater once more. The endless string of frantic questions reached her ears as she swam through the dark water.

"Are you all right?"

"What happened?"

"How did you get out?"

She reached the far edge of the lake, where Meris had melted another hole for her, and climbed onto the bank, wondering if she would ever see the boy again.

A few weeks later the ice melted for good and the fragrance of spring filled the air. Nerine spent her days gathering food in the woods and floating in the warming lake waters. She did not speak of the boy who had fallen through the ice, but she thought of him often. The nymphs, who suspected this, argued about it amongst themselves. Meris maintained that all humans were dangerous and should be avoided at any cost, but Marni, the second sister, was the most curious of the three, and she looked for opportunities to reunite Nerine with her mysterious stranger.

Marni got her chance one sunny afternoon when she saw the boy riding out on a hunt accompanied by two hounds. Marni had dominion over all the creatures of the lake, so with a few whispered words she drew a large school of fish toward the water's surface. Immediately, a flock of geese descended upon the water to devour the fish. In the distance, the boy's dogs caught the scent of the birds and raced toward the lake.

Nerine was sitting on the bank watching the geese when two massive hunting dogs burst through the trees. When they saw Nerine they forgot all about the geese and ran toward her instead. Nerine mistook their panting mouths and exposed fangs for aggression; her heart filled with fear and she leapt to her feet. She heard the dogs right behind her—she could almost feel them nipping at her heels—and scrambled up the nearest tree. Terrified, she looked down at the dogs, which were standing with their front paws on the tree trunk and howling loudly.

"Go away!" she cried, clinging to the slender branches. Then she heard hoofbeats and a loud whistle, and the dogs darted out of sight.

"What have you got there?" she heard a boy's voice call. "I'm guessing it's not a deer, unless stags have suddenly learned to climb trees…"

Nerine's eyes widened as the boy came into view, the very same boy she had pulled from the water. He dismounted from his horse and looked up through the budding leaves. "Oh," he said in surprise. "I'm so sorry. Don't be afraid, let me help you down from there."

He held out his hand and Nerine lowered herself from her high perch. The boy lifted her down from the tree and made sure she was steady before letting go. "Are you hurt?" he asked her. "I promise the dogs aren't violent; they're just easily excited."

Nerine shook her head. "No, I'm fine."

"Are you lost?" said the boy. "Perhaps I can help you find your way home."

Nerine laughed. "This is my home."

"You live here?" said the boy, looking around.

"For as long as I can remember."

The boy stared at her for a moment, frowning slightly. "You look so familiar to me…" he said quietly. Then his eyes lit up. "The lake! That's where I know you from. You're the one who pulled me from beneath the ice. I was starting to think I had dreamed you. What is your name?"

"Nerine," she said.

The boy swept a low bow. "I am Prince Gabriel," he said, "and I am eternally in your debt. Tell me, brave Nerine, is there anything I can do to begin to show my gratitude?"

Nerine's pale cheeks flushed. "Well," she said, eyeing the prince's hunter, "I must say, I have always wanted to ride a horse."

Over the coming weeks Nerine and Prince Gabriel spent much of their time together. She learned to ride and dance and hunt, and the prince marveled at her skill in the water. Never before had he seen someone catch a fish with her bare hands or swim with such speed. Aware of her great shyness, he introduced her gradually to his friends and companions, and soon Nerine no longer felt so alone. The nymphs disapproved, of course, for though Nerine was obviously fond of the prince, he was still human. Still, out of their great affection for Nerine they kept the waters of the lake cool and gentle, and chased away any snapping turtles who might threaten their dear child.

One night, after a splendid afternoon of feeding goslings with Nerine, Prince Gabriel returned home to find his grandfather enjoying a late supper in the banquet hall. He was surprised to see his grandfather; he had been away on summer progress and wasn't due home until August. Prince Gabriel bowed in greeting and sat down beside him.

"You look quite spent, Gabriel," said his grandfather. "I hope the summer has treated you well so far."

"It has, sir," Gabriel replied, grinning.

"Excellent," said his grandfather. "Any news I should know about?"

Prince Gabriel shook his head. "No sir, none that I can think of."

His grandfather raised one bushy white eyebrow. "Are you certain?" he said. "Because from the servants' constant whispers it sounds as though you've devoted much of your time to a mysterious young lady."

Prince Gabriel shifted in his seat, blushing. "Oh, right," he said, embarrassed. "Yes, she's quite extraordinary. In fact, I think I'm falling in love with her."

"Marvelous. And what's the blessed young lady's name?"

"Nerine," said the prince. "Beautiful, isn't it? She lives at the far end of the lake."

"I see," said his grandfather. He put down his knife and fork and stood up. "I am glad for you, Gabriel, and I know your mother and father would be too if they were still alive. Now kindly excuse me, I just remembered a letter I need to write tonight."

Prince Gabriel's grandfather walked to his study, his heart pounding from the news he had just heard. He pulled out a sheet of heavy paper and dipped his pen in the inkwell. He wrote quickly, the nib of the pen scratching the paper as the words covered the page. When he finished, he folded it and sealed it with wax. He called for a messenger, and ordered that the letter be delivered at once to the king and queen across the lake, who had lost their daughter seventeen years before. The Princess Nerine was found at last.

The next day Nerine and Prince Gabriel were walking along the edge of the lake, admiring the wildflowers, when they heard a loud trumpet blast. Nerine looked toward the woods, frowning in confusion as a parade of richly dressed men and women appeared. They rode on horseback and in carriages, their bright clothes reflecting in the glassy surface of the water. A young man broke off from the procession and rode ahead of the others, flanked by two heralds bearing standards. When he reached Nerine and Prince Gabriel he dismounted and bowed.

"Your Highness," he said to Nerine. "I am pleased to announce the arrival of your father and mother: the king and queen."

Nerine stared at him a moment, then looked up at Prince Gabriel. "What's going on?" she said. "Did he say they're my mother and father?"

Prince Gabriel had no answer for her. He watched, speechless, as the king and queen from across the lake dismounted their palfreys and rushed toward the girl at his side. Nerine dropped into an awkward curtsey, unsure of the proper etiquette. But the queen threw her arms around Nerine, drawing her into a crushing hug and abandoning etiquette altogether. Tears ran down the queen's face as she clutched her long-lost daughter.

"At last!" she cried. "I have my little girl again at last!" She pulled back and wiped her eyes. "Oh, Nerine, look how beautiful you've become. Such a lovely smile. I thought I would never see you again, and here you are."

Nerine shook her head. "I'm afraid there's been a mistake, Your Majesty. I live here—at the lake. I always have. I'm not a princess."

The king swept her up into his arms. "But you are, my darling. King Benedict wrote us himself. He was our greatest ally in our search for you. He never forgot your name, and when his grandson spoke of you the king knew you were the lost princess." He kissed Nerine's forehead and wrung Prince Gabriel's hand. "You have done a great thing, young man. Thank you for bringing our daughter back to us."

Prince Gabriel opened his mouth to protest, but stopped when the queen drew her daughter into another tight embrace. "We will feast tonight to celebrate your return," the queen trilled happily. "And we must get you out of those rags. I'll send for my dressmaker as soon as we reach the castle."

More men and women swarmed around the reunited royal family, and before Nerine knew what was happening she found herself seated in an ornate carriage with the king and queen. Their eager words fell muffled on her ears as the lake vanished around the corner. She hoped to see the nymphs rise out of the water and bid her farewell, but the water remained resolutely still.

That night Nerine sat at the center of the endless banquet table, her parents on either side. She had spent the entire afternoon preparing for her first public appearance, and now she was quite exhausted and uncomfortable. The maids had washed her with rosewater and combed her hair until it shone. They buffed and polished her fingernails and laced her into a corset so tight she thought she might faint. The dress the queen had chosen for her was the same color of the midnight sky, but the fabric was heavy and Nerine kept tripping over the long skirt.

When dinner was served Nerine scarcely touched her plate. Not because the food wasn't wonderful—the aroma of the roasted duck and warm bread alone made her mouth water—but because she felt so nervous. Everyone spoke gently to her, welcoming her back to the castle and wishing her well, but Nerine was so overwhelmed that she just smiled and hoped she wouldn't say anything foolish.

The last empty pudding dish was finally cleared from the table, and the musicians struck up a slow waltz. Nerine knew from the maids' warnings that she would be expected to dance, so she was relieved to see Prince Gabriel approaching instead of a stranger.

"Would you grant me the honor of a dance, Princess?" he asked.

Nerine answered by putting her hand in his. Prince Gabriel led her to the dance floor and they began to waltz. They talked quietly as they danced; Prince Gabriel assured Nerine he had no prior knowledge of his grandfather's letter, and Nerine confessed that she wasn't sure how she liked the life of a princess. More than anything, she told him, she wanted to see her aunts.

"I miss them so much," she said. "They raised me—I don't know what I'll do without them. I just wish I could tell them goodbye."

Prince Gabriel thought for a moment. "Perhaps there's a way you can," he said. "Do you know how to get back to the lake?" Nerine nodded, and he continued. "Excuse yourself in ten minutes and we'll meet there. You'll have plenty of time to talk to them and we'll be back before anyone notices we're gone."

"You don't mind going with me?" said Nerine.

"I'm happy to," he replied. The waltz ended and he kissed her hand. "I'll see you at the lake, Princess Nerine." They smiled at each other, delighting in their secret plan.

Unfortunately, the plan was not as secretive as they'd hoped. In the corner, listening to every word the pair exchanged, stood the sorceress. She had been fuming ever since Nerine's triumphant return to the castle, and seeing the princess enjoying herself only added to her rage. For seventeen years she'd believed that fool of a nurse had drowned the baby; she only wished the nurse was still alive so she might destroy her in revenge.

But there was still another target that might satisfy her wrath. The sorceress fixed her eyes on Prince

Gabriel. He was the one who found Nerine—it was because of him that the sorceress no longer had a place in the royal line. Fire rose in her eyes. Prince Gabriel would suffer for his crime.

A plan began to form in the sorceress's mind. She snapped her fingers, disguising herself as a maid, and followed after Nerine.

"Princess!" she called. "I couldn't help overhearing your plan. I won't tell anyone, I promise. But I thought you might want to change into something more comfortable. Those fine clothes aren't suitable for outdoor travel."

Nerine smiled. "Thank you. That's very kind."

The sorceress helped Nerine into a simpler dress, and then excused herself from the princess's rooms. With another snap of her fingers she assumed the appearance of Princess Nerine, still dressed in all her finery. She slipped out of the castle and rushed to meet Prince Gabriel at the lake.

She spotted him near the water's edge, his face glowing in the bright moonlight. She snapped her fingers again and a cup filled with steaming, sweet-smelling potion appeared in her hand. The sorceress approached Prince Gabriel and gave him a serene smile.

"I hope I haven't kept you waiting long," she said with Nerine's voice. "Please accept this as my apology. It will keep you warm on this cool night."

The sorceress watched with eager eyes as Prince Gabriel lifted the cup in a toast and began to drink. The taste pleased him, as the sorceress knew it would, and he eagerly gulped it until the cup was dry. For a moment the prince felt nothing but satisfaction. Then he felt a curious burning sensation in his throat. He turned to ask Nerine what the drink had contained, but saw the sorceress instead. Crippled with agony, Prince Gabriel fell to his knees. The burning sensation increased, filling his insides and spreading from his scalp to his toes. Fire seemed to run through his veins instead of blood. He collapsed fully to the ground, gasping for air.

Just then, Nerine arrived at the lake. When she saw Prince Gabriel she rushed to his side.

"Gabriel!" she cried. She put her cool hand on his cheek, but his skin was so hot it burned her hand to touch him. Blood seeped from the cracks in his white lips, and his eyes had lost the ability to focus. Nerine heard a ringing laugh behind her. She whirled around and saw the sorceress.

"Who are you?" Nerine asked with alarm. "What have you done to him?"

"I am the woman who was supposed to be queen," said the sorceress, "until this wretched fool brought you back to the castle and ruined the plan I put in place seventeen years ago." She smiled, enjoying the look of pain and confusion on Nerine's face. "I will take care of you in good time, water child, but only after you watch your beloved prince meet his heroic, dreadful end."

Desperate, Nerine grabbed the cup from where it had fallen and ran to the edge of the lake. She filled it with water and rushed back to Prince Gabriel. She pried his fiery lips open and lifted the cup.

"Just try to swallow," she instructed. But instead of pouring into Prince Gabriel's mouth, the water flew back to the lake, as though pulled by a magnet.

Nerine returned to the lake and tried again. By the time she reached Prince Gabriel the skin on his face was puckered like a dried apple and he couldn't open his eyes. Nerine's hand shook as she put the cup to his lips a second time. Again, the water flew back to the lake.

Nerine's eyes filled with tears as she made her third attempt. She knelt over Prince Gabriel; her tears fell on his face and evaporated into little puffs of steam, accompanied by a horrific sizzling sound. At any moment there would be nothing left of Prince Gabriel but a pile of ashes.

With a cry of frustration, Nerine threw down the cup and returned to the water a fourth time. She scooped up the cold water with her hands, intending to carry it back to Prince Gabriel, but the water just seeped through her fingers and returned to the lake. The sorceress watched with glee as Nerine sank onto the muddy bank, her face buried in her arms.

"I came to say goodbye," Nerine said quietly. She knew the nymphs could hear her, even though they remained hidden in the deep waters. "You know I would never leave by choice. I would stay here forever if I could. Don't punish him because of me."

She heard a splash, and lifted her head to see two small waves form in the water. The waves sped toward each other and clapped together; the resulting spray revealed Marissa, the third nymph. As the eldest sister she was the most powerful, controlling the flow of every drop of water in the lake. She looked at Nerine, her eyes empty of emotion.

Nerine's voice shook. "Help him, Aunt Marissa, please," she said.

The sorceress laughed. "You're wasting valuable time," she called. "You know as well as I do that a water nymph would never help a human."

Nerine ignored her. She had not forgotten how Meris had melted the ice and saved Prince Gabriel from drowning, and how Marni had used the fish to draw his hunting dogs to the lake. True, Marissa was more stern and serious than her younger sisters, but she was also fair and just. Nerine gathered her courage and looked up at the water nymph.

"Please don't let him die," she said.

"Give me a reason why I shouldn't," said Marissa. "He is, after all, only a human. What use is he to you?"

Nerine wiped her eyes and whispered, "I love him."

Marissa said nothing. A strong breeze picked up, scattering the spray back into the lake. Nerine waited, unsure if her dear aunt had even heard her plea. She staggered to her feet and returned to Prince Gabriel, who was barely clinging to life. She took his hand, and though the scorching heat made her skin burn, she did not care. She kissed his papery lips and tried to summon the will to say goodbye.

Suddenly, a great rushing sound filled the air. Nerine looked over her shoulder and saw all the water in the lake gather at the far side, then crash toward them in a wave so high it seemed to touch the stars. Nerine's heart pounded as she held tightly to Prince Gabriel, afraid he might be swept away. The water swirled around them, chilled to the perfect temperature by Meris. Marni placed thick leaves from her underwater plants over Prince Gabriel's eyes, and instructed her fish to soothe his skin with their cool scales. The color slowly returned to Prince Gabriel's cheeks, and only then did Marissa drew the water back to its rightful place in the lake. She even pretended not to notice when the sorceress was accidentally caught up in the wave and vanished beneath the surface of the water, never to be seen again.

In the coming years Nerine returned to the lake many times, though she never saw her beloved aunts again. Gabriel assured her that it wasn't for lack of love, and he was right. To this very day, if you happen to visit that lake in the dead of night, you might see a trio of water nymphs sitting on the bank and gazing at the spot where they once found a precious little baby.

About the author

N.C. Sellars began writing in college and hasn't stopped since. She loves traveling, cooking, and wandering the aisles of craft stores. She lives in South Carolina with her family.

Write to her at:

N.C. Sellars c/o Eskar Books

1140 Woodruff Road

Ste 106 #141

Greenville, SC 29607

Or email her at:

ncsellarsbooks@gmail.com

Keep an eye out for the

author's newest novel:

Kore's Field

A Greek myth brought to life

by

N.C. Sellars

Coming Spring 2018